# THE LAKE OF SOULS

## THE SAGA OF DARREN SHAN
### BOOK 10

*Other titles by*
# DARREN SHAN

## THE SAGA OF DARREN SHAN

## THE DEMONATA

*\*Also available on audio*

# DARREN SHAN

## THE LAKE OF SOULS

THE SAGA OF DARREN SHAN
BOOK 10

HarperCollins *Children's Books*

Hunt for Darren Shan on the web at
www.darrenshan.com

First published in Great Britain by HarperCollins *Children's Books* 2003
This edition published 2009
HarperCollins*Children'sBooks* is a division of HarperCollins*Publishers* Ltd,
77-85 Fulham Palace Road, Hammersmith,
London W6 8JB

The HarperCollins website address is:
www.harpercollins.co.uk

1

ISBN-13   978 0 00 794558 0

Printed and bound in England by
Clays Ltd, St Ives plc

For:

Bas — you steer my vaparetto!

OBE's

(Order of the Bloody Entrails) to:
Nate — the Sheffield Shanster Seer!

Banshee Babes:
Zoë Clarke & Gillie Russell

Global Grotesques:
the Christopher Little Clan

# PROLOGUE

DEATH WAS on the cards that day, but would it be ours or the panther's?

Black panthers are really leopards. If you look closely, you can see faint spots blended into their fur. But trust me — unless it's in a zoo, you don't ever want to be that close to a panther! They're one of nature's greatest killers. They move silently and speedily. In a one-on-one fight they'll almost always come out on top. You can't outrun them, since they're faster than you, and you can't out-climb them, because they can climb too. The best thing is to stay out of their way completely, unless you're an experienced big game hunter and have come packing a rifle.

Harkat and I had never hunted a panther before, and our best weapons were a few stone knives and a long, round-ended stick that served as a club. Yet there we were, on the edge of a pit which we'd dug the day before, watching a deer we'd captured and were using as bait, waiting for a panther.

We'd been there for hours, hidden in a bush, clutching our humble weapons close to our sides, when I spotted something long and black through the cover of the surrounding trees. A whiskered nose stuck out from around a tree and sniffed the air testingly — the panther. I nudged Harkat gently and we watched it, holding our breath, stiff with fright. After a few seconds the panther turned and padded away, back into the gloom of the jungle.

Harkat and I discussed the panther's retreat in whispers. I thought the panther had sensed a trap and wouldn't return. Harkat disagreed. He said it would come back. If we withdrew further, it might advance fully the next time. So we wriggled backwards, not stopping until we were almost at the end of the long stretch of bush. From here we could only vaguely see the deer.

A couple of hours passed. We said nothing. I was about to break the silence and suggest we were wasting our time, when I heard a large animal moving. The deer was jumping around wildly. There was a throaty growl. It came from the far side of the pit. That was great — if the panther attacked the deer from there, it might fall straight into our trap and be killed in the pit. Then we wouldn't have to fight it at all!

I heard twigs snap as the panther crept up on the deer. Then there was a loud snapping sound as a heavy body crashed through the covering over the pit and landed heavily on the stakes we'd set in the bottom. There was a ferocious howl, followed by silence.

Harkat slowly got to his feet and stared over the bush at the pit. I stood and stared with him. We glanced at each other. I said uncertainly, "It worked."

"You sound like you didn't … expect it to," Harkat grinned.

"I didn't," I laughed, and started towards the pit.

"Careful," Harkat warned. "It could still be alive."

Stepping in front of me, he moved off to the left and signalled for me to go right. Raising my knife, I circled away from Harkat, then we slowly closed on the pit from opposite directions.

Harkat was a few steps ahead of me, so he saw into the pit first. He stopped, confused. A couple of seconds later, I saw why. A body lay impaled on the stakes, blood dripping from its many puncture wounds. But it wasn't the body of a panther — it was a red baboon.

"I don't understand," I said. "That was a panther's growl, not a monkey's."

"But how did…" Harkat stopped and gasped. "The monkey's throat! It's been ripped open! The panther must—"

He got no further. There was a blur of movement in the upper branches of the tree closest to me. Whirling, I caught a very brief glimpse of a long, thick, pure black object flying through the air with outstretched claws and gaping jaws — then the panther was upon me, roaring triumphantly.

Death was on the cards that day.

# CHAPTER ONE

*Six months earlier.*

THE WALK up the tunnels, coming off the back of our battle with the vampaneze, was slow and exhausting. We left Mr Crepsley's charred bones in the pit where he'd fallen. I'd meant to bury him, but I hadn't the heart for it. Steve's revelation — that he was the Lord of the Vampaneze — had floored me, and now nothing seemed to matter. My closest friend had been killed. My world had been torn asunder. I didn't care whether I lived or died.

Harkat and Debbie walked beside me, Vancha and Alice Burgess slightly in front. Debbie used to be my girlfriend, but now she was a grown woman, whereas I was stuck in the body of a teenager — the curse of being a half-vampire who only aged one year for every five that passed. Alice was a police chief inspector. Vancha had kidnapped her when we'd been surrounded by police. She and Debbie had taken part in the fight with the vampaneze. They'd both fought well. A shame it had been for nothing.

We'd told Alice and Debbie all about the War of the Scars. Vampires exist, but not the murderous monsters of myth. We don't kill when we feed. But other night creatures do — the vampaneze. They broke away from the vampires six hundred years ago. They always drain their victims dry. Their skin has turned purple over the centuries, and their eyes and fingernails are red.

For a long time there'd been peace between the two clans. That ended when the Lord of the Vampaneze emerged. This vampaneze leader was destined to lead them into war against the vampires and destroy us. But if we found and killed him before he became a full-vampaneze, the war would go our way instead.

Only three vampires could hunt for the Vampaneze Lord (according to a powerful meddler called Desmond Tiny, who could see into the future). Two were Vampire Princes, Vancha March and me. The other had been Mr Crepsley, the vampire who'd blooded me and been like a father to me. He'd faced the person we thought was the Vampaneze Lord earlier that night and killed him. But then Steve sent Mr Crepsley tumbling to his death in a pit of flame-tipped stakes — shortly before he let me know that the person Mr Crepsley killed was an impostor, and that Steve himself was the Vampaneze Lord.

It didn't seem possible that Mr Crepsley was dead. I kept expecting a tap on my shoulder, and the tall orange-haired vampire to be standing behind me when I turned, grinning wickedly, his long facial scar glinting as he held up a torch, asking where we thought we were going without him. But the tap never came. It couldn't. Mr Crepsley was dead. He'd never come back.

Part of me wanted to go mad with rage, seize a sword and storm off after Steve. I wanted to track him down and drive a stake through his rotten excuse for a heart. But Mr Crepsley had warned me not to devote myself to revenge. He said it would warp and destroy me if I gave in to it. I knew in my soul that there was unfinished business between Steve and me, that our paths would cross again. But for the time being I pushed him from my thoughts and mourned for Mr Crepsley.

Except I couldn't really mourn. Tears wouldn't come. As much as I wanted to howl and sob with grief, my eyes remained dry and steely. Inside, I was a broken, weeping wreck, but on the outside I was cold, calm and collected, as though I hadn't been affected by the vampire's death.

Ahead, Vancha and Alice came to a halt. The Prince looked back, his wide eyes red from crying. He looked pitiful in his animal skins, with his filthy bare feet and wild hair, like an overgrown, lost child. "We're almost at the surface," he croaked. "It's still day. Will we wait here for dark? If we're spotted..."

"Don't care," I mumbled.

"I don't want to stay here," Debbie sobbed. "These tunnels are cruel."

"And I have to inform my people that I'm alive," Alice said, then frowned and picked dried blood flecks from her pale white hair. "Though I don't know how I'm going to explain it to them!"

"Tell the truth," Vancha grunted.

The Chief Inspector grimaced. "Hardly! I'll have to think up some—" She stopped. A figure had appeared out of the darkness ahead of us, blocking the path.

Cursing, Vancha ripped loose a shuriken — throwing stars he kept strapped in belts around his chest — and prepared to launch it.

"Peace, Vancha," the stranger said, raising a hand. "I am here to help, not harm."

Vancha lowered his shuriken and muttered in disbelief, "*Evanna?*"

The woman ahead of us clicked her fingers and a torch flared into life overhead, revealing the ugly witch we'd travelled with earlier in the year, while we were searching for the Lord of the Vampaneze. She hadn't changed. Short thick muscles, long untidy hair, pointed ears, a tiny nose, one brown eye and one green (the colours kept shifting from left to right), hairy body, long sharp nails and yellow ropes tied tight around her body instead of clothes.

"What are you doing … here?" Harkat asked, his large green eyes filled with suspicion — Evanna was a neutral in the War of the Scars, but could help or hinder those on either side, depending on her mood.

"I came to bid Larten's spirit farewell," the witch said. She was smiling.

"You don't look too cut up about it," I remarked without emotion.

She shrugged. "I foresaw his death many decades ago. I did my crying for him then."

"You knew he'd die?" Vancha growled.

"I wasn't certain, but I guessed he would perish," she said.

"Then you could have stopped it!"

"No," Evanna said. "Those with the ability to sense the currents of the future are forbidden to interfere. To save Larten, I'd have had to abandon the rules I live by, and if that happened, all chaos would break loose."

The witch stretched out a hand, and even though she was many metres away from Vancha, her fingers cupped his chin tenderly. "I was fond of Larten," she said softly. "I hoped I was wrong. But I couldn't take it upon myself to spare him. His fate wasn't mine to decide."

"Then whose was it?" Vancha snapped.

"His own," Evanna replied steadily. "*He* chose to hunt for the Lord of the Vampaneze, to enter the tunnels, to fight on the platform. He could have walked away from his responsibilities — but he chose not to."

Vancha glared at the witch a moment longer, then lowered his gaze. I saw fresh tears splash in the dust at his feet. "My apologies, Lady," he muttered. "I don't blame you. I'm just so fired up with hatred…"

"I know," the witch said, then studied the rest of us. "You must come with me. I have things to tell you, and I'd rather talk on the outside — the air here is rank with treachery and death. Will you spare me a few hours of your time?" She glanced at Alice Burgess. "I promise I won't keep you long."

Alice sniffed. "I guess a few hours can't make much of a difference."

Evanna looked at Harkat, Debbie, Vancha and me. We shared a glance, then nodded and followed the witch up the last stretch of the tunnels, leaving the darkness and the dead behind.

Evanna gave Vancha a thick deer hide to drape over his head and shoulders, to block out the rays of the sun. Trailing after the witch, we moved quickly through the streets. Evanna must have cast a spell to hide us, because people didn't notice us, despite our blood-stained faces and clothes. We ended up outside the city, in a small forest, where Evanna had prepared a camp amidst the trees. At her offer, we sat and tucked into the berries, roots and water she'd set out for us.

We ate silently. I found myself studying the witch, wondering why she was here — if she'd really come to say goodbye to Mr Crepsley, she'd have gone down to where his body lay in the pit. Evanna was Mr Tiny's daughter. He had created her by mixing the blood of a vampire with that of a wolf. Vampires and vampaneze were barren – we couldn't have children – but Evanna was supposed to be able to bear a child by a male of either clan. When we met her shortly after setting out to hunt the Vampaneze Lord, she'd confirmed Mr Tiny's prophecy – that we'd have four chances to kill the Lord – and added the warning that if we failed, two of us would die.

Vancha finished eating first, sat back and burped. "Speak," he snapped — he wasn't in the mood for formalities.

"You're wondering how many chances you've used up,"

Evanna said directly. "The answer is — three. The first was when you fought the vampaneze in the glade and let their Lord escape. The second, when you discovered Steve Leonard was a half-vampaneze and took him hostage — although you had several opportunities to kill him, they count as one. The third chance was when Larten faced him on the platform above the pit of stakes."

"That means we still have a shot at him!" Vancha hissed excitedly.

"Yes," Evanna said. "Once more the hunters will face the Vampaneze Lord, and on that occasion the future will be decided. But that confrontation will not come in the near future. Steve Leonard has withdrawn to plot anew. For now, you may relax."

The witch turned to me and her expression softened. "It might not lighten your load," she said kindly, "but Larten's soul has flown to Paradise. He died nobly and earned the reward of the righteous. He is at rest."

"I'd rather he was here," I said miserably, gazing at the leaves of an overhanging tree, waiting for tears which still wouldn't come.

"What about the rest of the vampaneze?" Alice asked. "Are any of them still in my city?"

Evanna shook her head. "All have fled."

"Will they return?" Alice asked, and by the glint in her eyes I saw she was half hoping they would, so she could settle a few scores.

"No." Evanna smiled. "But I think it's safe to say that you will run into them again."

"I'd better," Alice growled, and I knew she was thinking of Morgan James, an officer of hers who'd joined the vampets. They were human allies of the vampaneze, who shaved their heads, daubed blood around their eyes, sported V tattoos above their ears, and dressed in brown uniforms.

"Is the nightmare over then?" Debbie asked, wiping her dark cheeks clean. The teacher had fought like a tigress in the tunnels, but the events of the night had caught up with her and she was shivering helplessly.

"For you — for now," Evanna answered cryptically.

"What does that mean?" Debbie frowned.

"You and the Chief Inspector can choose to distance yourselves from the War of the Scars," Evanna said. "You can return to your ordinary lives and pretend this never happened. If you do, the vampaneze won't come after you again."

"Of course we'll return to our lives," Alice said. "What else can we do? We're not vampires. We don't have any further part to play in their war."

"Perhaps," Evanna said. "Or perhaps you'll think differently when you've had time to reconsider. You'll return to the city — you need time to reflect, and you have affairs to put in order — but whether or not you'll choose to stay..." Evanna's eyes flicked over Vancha, Harkat and me. "And where do you three wish to go?"

"I'm continuing after that monster, Leonard," Vancha said immediately.

"You may if you wish," Evanna shrugged, "but you'll be wasting your time and energy. Moreover, you will jeopardize your position. Although you are fated to confront him again, it's not written in stone — by pursuing him now, you might miss the final destined showdown."

Vancha cursed bitterly, then asked Evanna where she suggested he should go.

"Vampire Mountain," she said. "Your clan should be told about the Vampaneze Lord. They must not kill him themselves – that rule still applies – but they can scout for him and point you in the right direction."

Vancha nodded slowly. "I'll call a temporary end to the fighting and set everyone searching for him. I'll flit for Vampire Mountain as soon as night falls. Darren — are you and Harkat coming?"

I looked at my fellow Prince, then down at the hard brown earth of the forest floor. "No," I said softly. "I've had all I can take of vampires and vampaneze. I know I'm a Prince and have duties to attend to. But I feel like my head's about to explode. Mr Crepsley meant more to me than anything else. I need to get away from it all, maybe for a while — maybe for ever."

"It's a dangerous time to cut yourself off from those who care for you," Vancha said quietly.

"I can't help that," I sighed.

Vancha was troubled by my choice, but he accepted it. "I don't approve – a Prince should put the needs of his people before his own – but I understand. I'll explain it to the others. Nobody will trouble you." He cocked an eyebrow at Harkat. "I suppose you'll be going with him?"

Harkat lowered the mask from his mouth (air was poisonous to the grey-skinned Little People) and smiled thinly. "Of course." Mr Tiny had resurrected Harkat from the dead. Harkat didn't know who he used to be, but he believed he could find out by sticking with me.

"Where will you go?" Vancha asked. "I can find you using the Stone of Blood, but it'll be easier if I have a rough idea of where you're heading."

"I don't know," I said. "I'll just pick a direction and..." I stopped as a picture flashed through my thoughts, of circus vans, snake-boys and hammocks. "The Cirque Du Freak," I decided. "It's the nearest place outside Vampire Mountain that I can call home."

"A good choice," Evanna said, and by the way her lips lifted at the edges, I realized the witch had known all along that I'd choose to return to the Cirque.

We went our separate ways as the sun was setting, even though we hadn't slept and were ready to drop with exhaustion. Vancha departed first, on his long trek to Vampire Mountain. He said little when leaving, but hugged me hard and hissed in my ear, "Be brave!"

"You too," I whispered back.

"We'll kill Leonard next time," he vowed.

"Aye," I grinned weakly.

He turned and ran, hitting flitting speed seconds later, vanishing into the gloom of the dusk.

Debbie and Alice left next, to return to the city. Debbie asked me to stay with her, but I couldn't, not as things stood. I needed to be by myself for a while. She wept and clutched me close. "Will you come back later?" she asked.

"I'll try," I croaked.

"If he doesn't," Evanna said, "you can always go looking for him." She handed a folded-up piece of paper to Alice Burgess. "Hold on to that. Keep it closed. When the two of you decide upon your course, open it."

The Chief Inspector asked no questions, just tucked the paper away and waited for Debbie to join her. Debbie looked at me pleadingly. She wanted me to go with her – or ask her to come with me – but there was a huge ball of grief sitting cold and hard in my gut. I couldn't think of anything else right now.

"Take care," I said, turning aside and breaking eye contact.

"You too," she croaked, then sobbed loudly and stumbled away. With a quick "Goodbye", Alice hurried after her, and the two women slipped through the trees, back to the city, supporting one another as they went.

That left just me, Harkat and Evanna.

"Any idea where the Cirque's playing?" the witch asked. We shook our heads. "Then it's lucky that I do and am going there," she smiled. Standing between us, she looped her arms around my left arm and Harkat's right, and led us through the forest, away from the city and its underground caverns of death, back to where my voyage into the night first started — the Cirque Du Freak.

CHAPTER TWO

# CHAPTER TWO

ALEXANDER RIBS was sleeping in a large tyre hanging from a tree. He always slept curled up — it kept his body supple and made it easier for him to twist and contort when he was performing. Normally he kept the tyre on a special stand in his caravan, but occasionally he'd drag it outside and sleep in the open. It was a cold night for sleeping outdoors — the middle of a wintry November — but he had a thick, fur-lined body-bag to keep the chill out.

As Alexander snored musically a young boy crept towards him, a cockroach in his right hand, with the intention of dropping it into Alexander's mouth. Behind him, his older brother and younger sister looked on with impish glee, urging him forward with harsh hand gestures whenever he paused nervously.

As the boy neared the tyre and held up the cockroach, his mother — always alert to mischief — stuck her head out of a nearby tent, ripped her left ear off and threw it at him. It spun through the air like a boomerang and knocked the cockroach from the boy's pudgy fingers. Yelping, he raced back to his brother and sister, while Alexander slept on, unaware of his narrow escape.

"Urcha!" Merla snapped, catching her ear as it circled back, then reattaching it to her head. "If I catch you bothering Alexander again, I'll lock you in with the Wolf Man until morning!"

"Shancus made me do it!" Urcha whined, receiving a dig in the ribs from his older brother.

"I don't doubt he put you up to it," Merla growled, "but you're old enough to know better. Don't do it again. Shancus!" she added. The snake-boy looked at his mother innocently. "If Urcha or Lilia get into trouble tonight, I'll hold you responsible."

"I didn't do anything!" Shancus shouted. "They're always—"

"Enough!" Merla cut him short. She started towards her children, then saw me sitting in the shadow of the tree next to the one Alexander Ribs was hanging from. Her expression softened. "Hello, Darren," she said. "What are you doing?"

"Looking for cockroaches," I said, managing a short smile. Merla and her husband, Evra Von — a snake-man and one of my oldest friends — had been very kind to me since I'd arrived a couple of weeks earlier. Though I found it hard to respond to their kindness in my miserable mood, I made as much of an effort as I could.

"It's cold," Merla noted. "Shall I fetch you a blanket?"

I shook my head. "It takes more than a slight frost to chill a half-vampire."

"Well, would you mind keeping an eye on these three as long as you're outside?" she asked. "Evra's snake is moulting. If you can keep the kids out of the way, it'd be a real help."

"No problem," I said, rising and dusting myself down as she went back inside the tent. I walked over to the three Von children. They gazed up at me uncertainly. I'd been unusually solemn since returning to the Cirque Du Freak, and they weren't quite sure what to make of me. "What would you like to do?" I asked.

"Cockroach!" Lilia squealed. She was only three years old, but looked five or six because of her rough, coloured scales. Like Shancus, Lilia was half-human, half-snake. Urcha was an ordinary human, though he wished he could be like the other two, and sometimes glued painted scraps of tinfoil to his body, driving his mother wild with exasperation.

"No more cockroaches," I said. "Anything else?"

"Show us how you drink blood," Urcha said, and Shancus hissed at him angrily.

"What's wrong?" I asked Shancus, who'd been named in my honour.

"He's not supposed to say that," Shancus said, slicking back his yellow-green hair. "Mum told us not to say anything about vampires — it might upset you."

I smiled. "Mums worry about silly things. Don't worry — you can say whatever you like. I don't mind."

"Can you show us how you drink then?" Urcha asked again.

"Sure," I said, then spread my arms, pulled a scary face, and made a deep groaning noise. The children shrieked with delight and ran away. I plodded after them, threatening to rip their stomachs open and drink all their blood.

Although I was able to put on a merry display for the kids, inside I felt as empty as ever. I still hadn't come to terms with Mr Crepsley's death. I was sleeping very little, no more than an hour or two most nights, and I'd lost my appetite. I hadn't drunk blood since leaving the city. Nor had I washed, changed out of my clothes, cut my nails – they grew quicker than a human's – or cried. I felt hollow and lost, and nothing in the world seemed worthwhile.

When I'd arrived at the Cirque, Mr Tall had spent the day locked in his trailer with Evanna. They emerged late that night and Evanna took off without a word. Mr Tall checked that Harkat and I were OK, then set us up with a tent, hammocks and anything else we required. Since then he'd spent a lot of time talking with me, recounting tales of Mr Crepsley and what the pair of them had got up to in the past. He kept asking me to chip in with my own recollections, but I could only smile faintly and shake my head. I found it impossible to mention the dead vampire's name without my stomach tightening and my head pulsing with pain.

I hadn't said much to Harkat lately. He wanted to discuss our friend's death but I couldn't talk about it, and kept turning him away, which upset him. I was being selfish, but I couldn't help it. My sorrow was all consuming and endless, cutting me off from those who cared and wished to help.

Ahead, the Von children stopped, grabbed twigs and pebbles, and threw them at me. I stooped to grab a stick, but as I did, my thoughts flashed back to that underground cavern and Mr Crepsley's face as he let go of Steve and crashed upon the fiery stakes. Sighing mournfully, I sat down in the middle of the clearing, taking no notice as the Vons covered me with moss and dirt and prodded me curiously. They thought this was part of the game. I hadn't the heart to tell them otherwise, so I just sat still until they grew bored and wandered away. Then I remained there, filthy and alone, as the night darkened and grew colder around me.

As another week dragged by, I withdrew further and further inside myself. I no longer answered people when they asked a question, only grunted like an animal. Harkat had tried talking me out of my mood three days earlier, but I swore at him and told him to leave me alone. He lost his temper and took a swipe at me. I could have ducked out of the way of his chunky grey fist, but I let him knock me to the ground. When he bent to help me up, I swatted his hand away. He hadn't spoken to me since.

Life went on as usual around me. The Cirque folk were excited. Truska — a lady who could grow a beard at will, then suck the hairs back into her face — had returned after an absence of several months. A big party was held after that night's performance to celebrate her return. There was much cheering and singing. I didn't attend. I sat by myself at the edge of camp, stony-faced and dry-eyed, thinking – as usual – about Mr Crepsley.

Late in the night, there was a tap on my shoulder. Glancing up, I saw Truska, smiling, holding out a slice of cake. "I know you feeling low, but I'm thinking you might like this," she said. Truska was still learning to speak English and often mangled her words.

"Thanks, but I'm not hungry," I said. "Good to see you again. How have you been?" Truska didn't answer. She stared at me a moment — then thrust the slice of cake into my face! "What the hell!" I roared, leaping to my feet.

"That what you get for being big moody-guts," Truska laughed. "I know you sad, Darren, but you can't sit round like grumpy bear all time."

"You don't know anything about it," I snapped. "You don't know what I'm feeling. Nobody does!"

She looked at me archly. "You think you the only one to lose somebody close? I had husband and daughter. They get killed by evil fishermen."

I blinked stupidly. "I'm sorry. I didn't know."

"Nobody here does." She sat beside me, brushed her long hair out of her eyes and gazed up at the sky. "That why I left home and joined with Cirque Du Freak. I hurted terrible inside and had to get away. My daughter was less than two years old when she die."

I wanted to say something but my throat felt as though there was a rope tied tight around it.

"The death of somebody you love is the second worst thing in world," Truska said softly. "Worst thing is letting it hurt you so much that you die too — inside. Larten's dead and I am sad for him, but if you go on as you are being, I will be sadder for you, because you will be dead too, even though your body lives."

"I can't help it," I sighed. "He was like a father to me, but I didn't cry when he died. I still haven't. I can't."

Truska studied me silently, then nodded. "It hard to live with sadness if you can't get it out with tears. Don't worry — you'll cry in end. Maybe you feel better when you do." Standing, she offered me a hand. "You is dirty and smelly. Let me help clean you up. It might help."

"I doubt it," I said, but followed her into the tent that Mr Tall had prepared for her. I wiped the traces of cake from around my face, undressed and wrapped a towel around myself while Truska filled a tub with hot water and layered it with scented oils. She left me to get in. I felt foolish stepping into the sweet-smelling water, but it was wonderful once I lay down. I stayed there for almost an hour.

Truska came in when I'd stepped out of the tub and dried myself. She'd taken my dirty clothes, so I had to keep a towel wrapped around my middle. She made me sit in a low chair and set about my nails with a pair of scissors and a file. I told her they wouldn't be any good — vampires have extra-tough nails — but she smiled and clipped the top of the nail off my right big toe. "These super-sharp scissors.

I know all about vampire nails — I sometimes cut Vancha's!"

When Truska was done with my nails, she trimmed my hair, then shaved me and finished off with a quick massage. When she stopped, I stood and asked where my clothes were. "Fire," she smirked. "They was rotten. I chucked them away."

"So what do you suggest I wear?" I grumbled.

"I have surprise," she said. Going to a wardrobe, she plucked forth brightly coloured clothes and draped them across the foot of her bed. I instantly recognized the bright green shirt, purple trousers and blue-gold jacket — the pirate costume I used to wear when I lived at the Cirque Du Freak.

"You kept them," I muttered, smiling foolishly.

"I told you last time you was here that I have them and would fix them so you can wear again, remember?"

It seemed like years since we'd stopped at the Cirque shortly before our first encounter with the Lord of the Vampaneze. Now that I cast my mind back, I recalled Truska promising to adjust my old costume when she had a chance.

"I wait outside," Truska said. "Put them on and call when you ready."

I took a long time getting into the clothes. It felt weird to be pulling them on after all these years. The last time I'd worn them, I'd been a boy, still coming to terms with being a half-vampire, unaware of how hard and unforgiving the world could be. Back then I thought the clothes looked cool, and I loved wearing them. Now they looked childish and silly to me, but since Truska had gone to the trouble of preparing them, I figured I'd better put them on to please her.

I called her when I was ready. She smiled as she entered, then went to a different wardrobe and came back with a brown hat adorned with a long feather. "I not have shoes your size," she said. "We get some later."

Pulling on the hat, I tilted it at an angle and smiled self-consciously at Truska. "How do I look?"

"See for yourself," she replied, and led me to a full-length mirror.

My breath caught in my throat as I came face to face with my reflection. It may have been a trick of the dim light, but in the fresh clothes and hat, with my clean-shaven face, I looked very young, like when Truska first kitted me out in this costume.

"What you think?" Truska asked.

"I look like a child," I whispered.

"That is partly the mirror," she chuckled. "It is made to take off a few years — very kind to women!"

Removing the hat, I ruffled my hair and squinted at myself. I looked older when I squinted — lines sprang up around my eyes, a reminder of the sleepless nights I'd endured since Mr Crepsley's death. "Thanks," I said, turning away from the mirror.

Truska put a firm hand on my head and swivelled me back towards my reflection. "You not finished," she said.

"What do you mean?" I asked. "I've seen all there is to see."

"No," she said. "You haven't." Leaning forward, she tapped the mirror. "Look at your eyes. Look deep in them, and don't turn away until you see."

"See what?" I asked, but she didn't answer. Frowning, I gazed into my eyes, reflected in the mirror, searching for anything strange. They looked the same as ever, a little sadder than usual, but...

I stopped, realizing what Truska wanted me to see. My eyes didn't just look sad — they were completely empty of life and hope. Even Mr Crepsley's eyes, as he died, hadn't looked that lost. I knew now what Truska meant when she said the living could be dead too.

"Larten not want this," she murmured in my ear as I stared at the hollow eyes in the mirror. "He love life. He want you to love it too. What would he say if he saw this alive-but-dead gaze that will get worse if you not stop?"

"He ... he..." I gulped deeply.

"Empty is no good," Truska said. "You must fill eyes, if not with joy, then with sadness and pain. Even hate is better than empty."

"Mr Crepsley told me I wasn't to waste my life on hate," I said promptly, and realized this was the first time I'd mentioned his name since arriving at the Cirque Du Freak. "Mr Crepsley," I said again, slowly, and the eyes in the mirror wrinkled. "Mr Crepsley," I sighed. "Larten. My friend." My eyelids were trembling now, and tears gathered at the edges. "He's dead," I moaned, turning to face Truska. "Mr Crepsley's dead!"

With that, I threw myself into her embrace, locked my arms around her waist, and wailed, finally finding the tears to express my grief. I wept long and hard, and the sun had risen on a new morning before I cried myself out and slid to the floor, where Truska slipped a pillow under my head and hummed a strange, sad tune as I closed my eyes and slept.

# CHAPTER THREE

IT WAS a cold but dry March — star-filled nights, frost-white dawns and sharp blue days. The Cirque Du Freak was performing in a large town situated close to a waterfall. We'd been there four nights already, and it would be another week before we moved on — lots of tourists were coming to our shows, as well as the residents of the town. It was a busy, profitable time.

In the months after I first cried in Truska's tent, I'd wept a lot for Mr Crepsley. It had been horrible — the slightest reminder of him could set me off — but necessary. Gradually the tearful bursts had lessened, as I came to terms with my loss and learnt to live with it.

I was lucky. I had lots of friends who helped. Truska, Mr Tall, Hans Hands, Cormac Limbs, Evra and Merla all talked me through the hard times, discussing Mr Crepsley with me, gently guiding me back to normality. Once I'd patched things up with Harkat and apologized for the way I'd treated him, I relied on the Little Person more than anyone else. We sat up many nights together, remembering Mr Crepsley, reminding each other of his personal quirks, things he'd said, expressions he'd favoured.

Now, months later, the tables had turned and *I* was doing the comforting. Harkat's nightmares had returned. He'd been suffering from agonizing dreams when we left Vampire Mountain at the start of our quest, dreams of wastelands, stake-filled pits and dragons. Mr Tiny said the dreams would worsen unless Harkat went with him to find out who he'd been before he died, but Harkat chose to accompany me instead on my hunt for the Vampaneze Lord.

Later, Evanna helped me stop his nightmares. But the witch said it was only a temporary solution. When the dreams resumed, Harkat would have to find out the truth about himself or be driven insane.

For the last month Harkat had been tormented every time he slept. He stayed awake as long as he could – Little People didn't need much sleep – but whenever he dozed off, the nightmares washed over him and he'd thrash and scream in his sleep. It had reached the stage where he had to be tied down when he slept — otherwise he stumbled through the camp, hitting out at imaginary monsters, causing damage to anything he encountered.

After five days and nights, he'd fallen asleep at the end of our latest show. I'd tied him down in his hammock, using strong ropes to strap his arms by his sides, and sat beside him while he tossed and moaned, wiping green beads of sweat from his forehead, away from his lidless eyes.

Finally, early in the morning, after hours of shrieking and straining, the cries stopped, his eyes cleared and he smiled weakly. "You can untie me … now. All done for tonight."

"That was a long one," I muttered, undoing the knots.

"That's the trouble with putting … sleep off so long," Harkat sighed, swinging out of his hammock. "I postpone the nightmares for a while, but I … sleep longer."

"Maybe you should try hypnosis again," I suggested. We'd done everything we could think of to ease Harkat's pain, asking all the performers and crew in the Cirque if they knew of a cure for nightmares. Mr Tall had tried hypnotizing him, Truska had sung to him while he slept, Rhamus Twobellies had rubbed a foul-smelling ointment over his head — all to no avail.

"No good," Harkat smiled tiredly. "Only one person can help — Mr Tiny. If he returns and shows me how to … find out who I was, the dreams … will hopefully stop. Otherwise…" He shook his squat, grey, neckless head.

After washing off the sweat in a barrel of cold water, Harkat accompanied me to Mr Tall's van, to learn our schedule for the day. We'd been doing a variety of odd jobs since hooking up with the Cirque, putting up tents, fixing broken seats and equipment, cooking and washing.

Mr Tall had asked me if I'd like to perform in the shows, as his assistant. I told him I didn't want to — it would have felt too weird being on stage without Mr Crepsley.

When we reported for duty, Mr Tall was standing in the doorway of his van, beaming broadly, his little black teeth shining dully in the early morning light. "I heard you roaring last night," he said to Harkat.

"Sorry," Harkat said.

"Don't be. I mention it only to explain why I didn't come to you straightaway with the news — I thought it best to let you sleep."

"What news?" I asked warily. In my experience, unexpected news was more often bad than good.

"You have visitors," Mr Tall chuckled. "They arrived late last night, and have been waiting impatiently." He stepped aside and waved us in.

Harkat and I shared an uncertain glance, then entered cautiously. Neither of us carried a weapon — there seemed to be no need while we travelled with the Cirque Du Freak — but we bunched our hands into fists, ready to lash out if we didn't like the look of our "visitors". Once we saw the pair sitting on the couch, our fingers relaxed and we bounded forward, excited.

"Debbie!" I yelled. "Alice! What are you doing here?"

Debbie Hemlock and Chief Inspector Alice Burgess rose to hug us. They were simply dressed in trousers and jumpers. Debbie had cut her hair since I last saw her. It was short and tightly curled. I didn't think it suited her, but I said nothing about it.

"How are you?" Debbie asked once I'd released her. She was studying my eyes quietly, checking me out.

"Better," I smiled. "It's been rough but I'm over the worst — touch wood."

"Thanks to his friends," Harkat noted wryly.

"What about you?" I asked the women. "Did the vampaneze return? How did you explain things to your bosses and friends?" Then, "What are you doing here?" I asked again, perplexed.

Debbie and Alice laughed at my confusion, then sat down and explained all that had happened since we parted in the forest outside the city. Rather than make a genuine report to her superiors, Alice claimed to have been unconscious the entire time since being kidnapped by Vancha March. It was a simple story, easy to stick to, and nobody had cause to disbelieve her.

Debbie faced rougher questioning — when the vampaneze told the police we were holding Steve Leonard, they also mentioned Debbie's name. She'd protested her innocence, said she only knew me as a student, and knew nothing at all about Steve. With Alice's support, Debbie's story was finally accepted and she was released. She'd been shadowed for a few weeks, but eventually the police left her to get on with her life.

The officials knew nothing of the battle that had taken place in the tunnels, or of the vampaneze, vampets and vampires who'd been busy in their city. As far as they were concerned, a group of killers – Steve Leonard, Larten Crepsley, Darren Shan, Vancha March and Harkat Mulds – were responsible for the murders. One escaped during their arrest. The others broke out of prison later and fled. Our descriptions had been circulated near and far, but we were no longer the problem of the city, and the people there didn't much care whether we'd been humans or vampires — they were just glad to be rid of us.

When a suitable period had passed, and interest in them dropped, Alice met Debbie and the pair discussed their bizarre brush with the world of vampires. Debbie had quit her job at Mahler's — she couldn't face work — and Alice was thinking about handing in her resignation too.

"It seemed pointless," she said quietly, running her fingers through her short white hair. "I joined the force to protect people. When I saw how mysterious and deadly the world really is, I no longer felt useful. I couldn't return to ordinary life."

Over a number of weeks, the women talked about what they'd experienced in the tunnels, and what to do with their lives. They both agreed that they couldn't go back to the way they'd been, but they didn't know how to reshape their futures. Then, one night, after a lot of drinking and talking, Debbie said something that would change their lives completely and give them a new, purposeful direction.

"I was worrying about the vampets," Debbie told us. "They seem more vicious than the vampaneze. Their masters have morals of a kind, but the vampets are just thugs. If the vampaneze win the war, it doesn't seem likely that the vampets will want to stop fighting."

"I agreed," Alice said. "I've seen their kind before. Once they develop a taste for battle, they never lose it. But without vampires to attack, they'll have to look elsewhere for prey."

"Humanity," Debbie said quietly. "They'll turn on humans if they get rid of all the vampires. They'll keep recruiting, growing all the time, finding weak, greedy people and offering them power. With the vampaneze behind them, I think they might pose a real threat to the world in the years to come."

"But we didn't think the vampires would worry about that," Alice said. "The vampaneze are the real threat to the vampire clan. The vampets are just a nuisance as far as vampires are concerned."

"That's when I said we needed to fight fire with fire." Debbie's face was stern, unusually so. "This is *our* problem. I said we needed to recruit humans to fight the vampets, now, before they grow too strong. I was speaking generally when I used 'our' and 'we', but as soon as I said it, I realized it wasn't general — it was personal."

"Victims wait for others to fight on their behalf," Alice said roughly. "Those who don't want to be victims fight for themselves."

By the time the sun rose, the pair had drawn up a plan to travel to Vampire Mountain, elicit the approval of the Princes, and build an army of humans to counter the threat of the vampets. Vampires and vampaneze don't use guns or bows and arrows – they make a vow when blooded never to avail of such weapons – but vampets aren't bound by such laws. Alice and Debbie's army wouldn't be bound by those laws either. With the help of the vampires they could track the vampets, then engage them on equal, vicious terms.

"We'd almost finished packing before the glaring flaw hit us," Debbie laughed. "We didn't know where Vampire Mountain was!"

That's when Alice recalled the piece of paper Evanna had given her. Returning to her apartment, where she'd stored it, she unfolded it and discovered directions to where the Cirque Du Freak was currently playing — here by the waterfall.

"But Evanna gave you that paper months ago!" I exclaimed. "How did she know where the Cirque would be?"

Alice shrugged. "I've tried not to think about that one. I'm just about OK with the notion of vampires, but witches who can foresee the future ... that's a step too far. I prefer to believe she checked with the guy who runs this place before she met us."

"Though that doesn't explain how she knew when we'd read the message," Debbie added with a wink.

"I suppose this means we're meant to ... guide you to Vampire Mountain," Harkat mused.

"Looks like it," Alice said. "Unless you've other plans?"

Harkat looked at me. I'd made it very clear when Mr Crepsley died that I didn't want anything to do with vampires for a while. This call was mine.

"I'm not keen on going back," I sighed. "It's still too soon. But for something this important, I guess I don't have much of a choice. As well as showing you the way, maybe I can act as the middle man between you and the Generals."

"We were thinking along those lines," Debbie smiled, leaning over to squeeze my hands. "We're not sure what the vampires will think of two human women turning up with an offer to build an army to help them. We know little of their ways or customs. We need someone to fill us in."

"I'm not sure the Princes will … accept your proposal," Harkat said. "Vampires have always fought their … own battles. I think they'll want to do the same now, even … if the odds are stacked against them."

"If they do, we'll fight the vampets without them," Alice snorted. "But they'd be fools to disregard us, and from what I've seen, vampires aren't foolish."

"It makes sense," I said. "Send humans to fight the vampets and leave the clan free to focus on the vampaneze."

"Since when did vampires do things … because they made sense?" Harkat chuckled. "But it's worth a try. I'll come with you."

"Oh no you won't," someone chortled behind us. Turning, startled, we saw that we'd been joined in the van by a third, uninvited guest, a short man with a savage leer. He was instantly recognizable and immediately unwelcome — *Mr Tiny!*

# CHAPTER FOUR

THE CREATOR of the Little People was dressed in his customary yellow suit and green Wellington boots. He eyed us though thick glasses and twirled a heart-shaped watch between the fingers of his left hand. He was small and pudgy, with pure white hair and a cruel, mocking smile.

"Hello boys," he greeted Harkat and me. "And *hello!* beautiful ladies." He winked rakishly at Debbie and Alice. Debbie smiled, but the ex-Chief Inspector was wary. Mr Tiny took a seat and removed a boot to empty dirt out of it. I saw the strange, six webbed toes I'd glimpsed once before. "I see you survived your run-in with Master Leonard," he drawled, putting the boot back on.

"No thanks to you," I sniffed angrily. "You knew Steve was the Lord of the Vampaneze. You could have told us."

"And spoilt the surprise?" Mr Tiny laughed. "I wouldn't have missed that fatal confrontation in the Cavern of Retribution for anything. I haven't enjoyed myself so much in years. The tension was unbearable, even though I guessed the outcome."

"You weren't in the cavern," I challenged him. "And you didn't *guess* the outcome — you *knew* how it would end!"

Mr Tiny yawned insolently. "I might not have been there physically," he said, "but I was there in spirit. As for knowing the final outcome — I didn't. I suspected Larten would fail, but I wasn't sure. He *could* have won.

"Anyhow," he said, clapping sharply. "That's in the past. We've other fish to fry." Looking at Harkat, he spun his watch so that it caught the light shining in the window of the van and reflected it into Harkat's round green eyes. "Been sleeping well, Master Mulds?"

Harkat stared straight back at his master and said blankly, "You know only too damn ... well that I haven't."

Mr Tiny tucked his watch away without taking his eyes off Harkat. "Time to find out who you used to be," he murmured. Harkat stiffened.

"Why now?" I asked.

"His nightmares have intensified. He must come with me and search for his true identity, or stay, go mad — and perish."

"Why can't you just tell him?" I prodded.

"Doesn't work that way," Mr Tiny said.

"Will I be gone long?" Harkat asked quietly.

"Oh yes," came the answer. "For ever, if things don't go well. It's not a case of simply finding out who you were and returning. The road is long and dangerous, and even if you struggle along to the end, there's no guarantee you'll make it back. But it's a road you must tread — unless you'd rather go loopy and die." Mr Tiny let out a fake sigh. "Poor Harkat — trapped between the devil and the deep blue sea."

"You're all heart," Harkat grumbled, then faced me with a look of disgust. "Looks like this is where ... we part company."

"I could come with you–" I began, but he cut me short with a wave of a rough grey hand.

"Forget it," he said. "You have to lead Debbie and ... Alice to Vampire Mountain. Not just to guide them, but to ... protect them — it's a hard trek."

"We could wait until you returned," Debbie said.

"No," Harkat sighed. "There's no telling how long ... I'll be gone."

I gazed helplessly at Harkat. He was my best friend, and I hated the thought of leaving him. But I loved Debbie and didn't want to abandon her.

"Actually," Mr Tiny purred, stroking the top of his heart-shaped watch, "I think young Shan *should* accompany you — assuming you value your life."

"What do you mean?" Harkat barked sharply.

Mr Tiny studied his fingernails and spoke with a deceptively light tone. "If Darren accompanies you, your chances of survival are fair. Alone, it's practically certain you'll fail."

My eyes narrowed hatefully. Mr Tiny had set Mr Crepsley and me on the trail of the Vampaneze Lord, knowing it was a journey bound to end in death. Now he wished to launch me on another.

"Darren's not coming," Harkat said as I opened my mouth to lay into Mr Tiny. "He has problems of his own … with the vampaneze. This is my quest, not his."

"Of course, dear boy," Mr Tiny simpered. "I fully understand, and if he chooses to go with the beautiful ladies, I won't say anything to stop him. But it would be terribly wrong of me not to let him know in advance the awful—"

"Stop!" Harkat snapped. "Darren goes with Debbie and … Alice. End of story."

"Harkat," I muttered uncertainly, "maybe we should—"

"No," he stopped me. "Your loyalty lies with the vampires. It's time you returned to the fold. I'll be OK on my own." And he turned away and wouldn't say anything more about it.

We broke camp before midday. Debbie and Alice had come well equipped, with ropes, thick jumpers, climbing boots, strong torches, lighters and matches, guns, knives, you name it! As a half-vampire, I didn't require any special tools. All I packed in my rucksack was a good strong knife and a change of clothes. I was wearing jeans, a shirt and a light jumper. Although Truska had gone to a lot of trouble restoring my pirate costume, I didn't feel comfortable in it — it was a child's outfit. I'd picked up more normal gear over the last few months. Truska didn't mind — she said she'd give the costume to Shancus or Urcha when they were older.

I didn't wear my shoes. The trek to Vampire Mountain was a solemn tradition among vampires. No shoes or climbing gear were allowed. Normally you weren't allowed to flit either.

In recent years, because of the War of the Scars, that rule had been relaxed. But the others still stood. Debbie and Alice thought I was crazy! It's hard for humans to understand the world of the creatures of the night.

One other thing I did take was my diary. I'd thought the diary lost for ever – it had been left behind in the city, along with the rest of my personal belongings – and was astonished when Alice produced it with a flourish.

"Where'd you get it?" I gasped, fingering the soft, crinkled cover of one of the several notepads that made up the diary.

"It was part of the evidence my officers collected after you were arrested. I sneaked it out before I quit the force."

"Did you read it?" I asked.

"No, but others did." She smiled. "They dismissed it as the fictional work of a lunatic."

I looked for Harkat before we left, but he was locked away in Mr Tall's van with Mr Tiny. Mr Tall came to the door when I knocked and said the Little Person was not receiving visitors. I called out "Goodbye" but there was no reply.

I felt lousy as we cleared the camp, having said farewell to Evra, Merla and my other friends. But Harkat had been firm about his wishes, and I knew it made more sense to go to Vampire Mountain and take my rightful place in the Hall of Princes again.

Debbie was delighted to have me back, and held on tight to my hand, telling me how excited she was – and a bit scared – to be heading for Vampire Mountain. She pumped me for information – what did vampires wear, did they sleep in coffins, could they turn into bats – but I was too distracted to answer in any great detail.

We'd walked two or three kilometres when I drew to a sudden halt. I was thinking about the times Harkat had saved my life — when he'd rescued me from the jaws of a savage bear, when he'd jumped into a pit during my Trials of Initiation and killed a wild boar as it was about to gouge me to death, the way he'd fought beside me, swinging his axe with speed and skill, when we'd taken on the vampaneze.

"Darren?" Debbie asked, gazing into my eyes, worried. "What's wrong?"

"He's got to go back," Alice answered for me. I stared at her and she smiled. "You can't ignore the obligations of friendship. Harkat needs you more than we do. Go help him, and catch us up later if you can."

"But he told me to leave," I muttered.

"Doesn't matter," Alice insisted. "Your place is with him, not us."

"No!" Debbie objected. "We can't find our way to the Mountain alone!"

Alice pulled a map out of her rucksack. "I'm sure Darren can point us in the right direction."

"No!" Debbie cried again, clutching me tight. "I'm afraid I'll never see you again if you leave!"

"I must," I sighed. "Alice is right — I have to help Harkat. I'd rather stay with you, but I'd feel like a traitor if I did."

There were hard tears in Debbie's eyes, but she blinked them back and nodded tensely. "OK. If that's the way you want it."

"It's the way it has to be," I said. "You'd do the same thing in my place."

"Possibly." She smiled weakly, then, hiding her feelings behind a businesslike façade, she grabbed the map off Alice, laid it on the ground and told me to ink in the route to Vampire Mountain.

I quickly outlined the easiest route, pointed out a couple of alternate paths in case the first was blocked, and told them how to find their way through the maze of tunnels which led up the inside of the Mountain to the Halls where the vampires lived. Then, without any long goodbyes, I kissed Debbie quickly and thrust the rucksack with my newly recovered diary into Alice's hands. I asked her to look after it for me.

I wished both women well, then turned and raced back for camp. I tried not to dwell on all that could happen to them on their way to the Mountain, and offered up a quick prayer to the gods of the vampires as I ran, asking them to watch over the ex-Chief Inspector and the teacher I loved.

I was on the edge of the camp when I spotted Mr Tiny and Harkat in an open field. In front of the pair stood a shimmering arched doorway, unconnected to anything else. The edges of the doorway glowed red. Mr Tiny also glowed, his suit, hair and skin pulsing a dark, vibrant, crimson shade. The space within the edges of the doorway was a dull grey colour.

Mr Tiny heard me coming, looked over his shoulder and smiled like a shark. "Ah — Master Shan! I thought you might turn up."

"Darren!" Harkat snapped furiously. "I told you not to come! I won't take you with ... me. You'll have to—"

Mr Tiny laid a hand on the Little Person's back and shoved him through the doorway. There was a grey flash, then Harkat disappeared. I could see the field through the grey veil of the doorway — but no sign of Harkat.

"Where's he gone?" I shouted.

"To search for the truth." Mr Tiny smiled, edged aside and gestured towards the glowing doorway. "Care to search with him?"

I stepped up to the doorway, gazing uneasily at the glowing red edges and the grey sheen between. "Where does this lead?" I asked.

"Another place," Mr Tiny answered obscurely, then laid a hand on my right shoulder and looked at me intently. "If you follow Harkat, you might never return. Think seriously about this. If you go with Harkat and die, you won't be here to face Steve Leonard when the time comes, and your absence might have terrible repercussions for vampires everywhere. Is your short, grey-skinned friend worth such an enormous risk?"

I didn't have to think twice about that. "Yes," I answered simply, and stepped through into unnatural, otherworldly greyness.

# CHAPTER FIVE

A SUN burnt brightly in the clear sky above the wasteland, highlighting the arid earth and bare rocky hills. A coarse red dust covered much of the land, choking the dry soil. When strong winds blew, the dust rose in sheets, making breathing almost impossible. At such times I pulled on one of Harkat's spare masks – it blocked out the worst of the grainy particles – and the two of us sought shelter and waited for calm to descend.

It had been two weeks – roughly – since Mr Tiny brought us to this desolate land and abandoned us. Two weeks crossing barren valleys and dead hills, where nothing lived except a few hardy lizards and insects, which we caught and ate whenever we could. They tasted disgusting but you can't be choosy if you're stranded in a desert without food or water.

Water was our main concern. Walking in the heat and dust was thirsty work, but water was in scarce supply and we didn't have any canteens to store it in when we found the occasional pool. We'd fashioned primitive containers from the skins of lizards, but they didn't hold much. We had to drink sparingly.

Harkat was angry with me for disobeying his wishes – he ranted at me nonstop for a few days – but his temper gradually abated. Although he hadn't thanked me for choosing to accompany him on his quest, I knew he was secretly grateful.

A fortnight earlier, Mr Tiny followed us through the doorway, which collapsed into dust after him. There'd been a brief moment of disorientation when I stepped through, a grey cloud obscuring my vision. As the cloud cleared, I saw that I was standing in a round, shallow, lifeless valley — and although it had been day when I stepped through the doorway, here it was night, albeit an uncommonly clear night, bright with a full moon and a sky filled with twinkling star clusters.

"Where are we?" Harkat asked, his large green eyes filled with wonder.

Mr Tiny tapped his nose. "That would be telling. Now, boys," he said, squatting and signalling us to squat beside him. He drew a simple compass in the dust at his feet, and pointed to one of the arrows. "That's west, as you'll see by the position of the sun tomorrow. Go in that direction until you come to the hunting grounds of a black panther. You have to kill the panther to find out where to go next."

Smiling, he stood and turned to leave.

"Wait!" I stopped him. "Is that all you're going to tell us?"

"What more would you like to know?" he asked politely.

"Loads!" I shouted. "Where are we? How did we get here? What happens if we walk east instead of west? How will Harkat find out who he used to be? And what the hell does a panther have to do with any of it?"

Mr Tiny sighed impatiently. "I thought you would have developed an appreciation for the unknown by now," he grumbled. "Don't you realize how exciting it is to set out on an adventure without any idea of what's coming next? I'd give my wellies and glasses to experience the world the way you do, as something strange and challenging."

"Forget the wellies and glasses!" I snapped. "Just give with some answers!"

"You can be very rude sometimes," Mr Tiny complained, but squatted again and paused thoughtfully. "There's much I can't and won't tell you. You'll have to discover for yourselves where we are — although it won't make much difference if you don't. You got here, obviously, through a mechanism either of magic or incredibly evolved technology — I'm not saying which. If you don't follow the trail west, you'll die, probably quite horribly. As for Harkat finding out who he is, and the panther…"

Mr Tiny considered the question in silence, before answering. "Somewhere on this world lies a lake — more a glorified pond, really — which I like to refer to as the Lake of Souls. In it you can glimpse the faces of many trapped souls, people whose spirits did not leave Earth when they died. The soul of the person Harkat used to be lies within. You must find the Lake, then fish for his soul. If you succeed, and Harkat learns and acknowledges the truth about himself, your quest will be complete and I'll see that you're guided safely home. If not..." He shrugged.

"How do we find this Lake ... of Souls?" Harkat asked.

"By following instructions," Mr Tiny said. "If you locate and kill the panther, you'll learn where to go next. You'll also discover a clue to your previous identity, which I've been gracious enough to toss in for free."

"Couldn't you just cut the crap and tell us?" I groaned.

"No," Mr Tiny said. He stood and looked down at us seriously. "But I'll say this much, boys — the panther's the least of your worries. Step warily, trust in your instincts, and never let your guard down. And don't forget," he added to Harkat, "as well as learning who you were, you must acknowledge it. I can't step in until you've admitted the truth out loud.

"Now," he smiled, "I really must be going. Places to be, things to do, people to torment. If you've further questions, they'll have to wait. Until next time, boys." With a wave, the short, mysterious man turned and left us, walking east until the darkness swallowed him, stranding us in the unnamed, alien land.

We found a small pool of water and drank deeply from it, sinking our heads into the murky liquid, ignoring the many tiny eels and insects. Harkat's grey skin looked like damp cardboard when he pulled up, having drunk his fill, but it swiftly resumed its natural colour as the water evaporated under the unforgiving sun.

"How far do you think we've come?" I groaned, stretching out in the shade of a prickly bush with small purple flowers. This was the first sign of vegetation we'd encountered, but I was too exhausted to display any active interest.

"I've no idea," Harkat said. "How long have we ... been travelling?"

"Two weeks — I think."

After the first hot day, we'd tried travelling by night, but the path was rocky and treacherous underfoot — not to mention hard on my bare feet! After stumbling many times, ripping our clothes and cutting ourselves, we elected to brave the blistering sun. I wrapped my jumper around my head to ward off the worst of the rays — the sun didn't affect Harkat's grey skin, though he sweated a lot — but while that prevented sunstroke, it didn't do much against sunburn. My upper body had been roasted all over, even through the material of my shirt. For a few days I'd been sore and irritable, but I'd recovered quickly — thanks to my healing abilities as a half-vampire — and the red had turned to a dark, protective brown. The soles of my feet had also hardened — I barely noticed the absence of shoes now.

"With all the climbing and back tracking we've ... had to do, we can't be making more than ... a couple of miles an hour," Harkat said. "Allowing for fourteen or fifteen hours of sunlight ... per day, we probably cover twenty-five or thirty miles. Over two weeks that's…" He frowned as he calculated. "Maybe four hundred in total."

I nodded feebly. "Thank the gods we're not human — we wouldn't have lasted a week at this pace, in these conditions."

Harkat sat up and tilted his head left, then right — the Little Person's ears were stitched under the skin of his scalp, so he had to cock his head at a sharp angle to listen intently. Hearing nothing, he focused his green eyes on the land around us. After a brief study of the area, he turned towards me. "Has the smell altered?" he asked. He didn't have a nose, so he relied on mine.

I sniffed the air. "Slightly. It doesn't smell as tangy as it did before."

"That's because there's less … dust," he said, pointing to the hills around us. "We seem to be leaving the … desert behind. There are a few plants and patches … of dry grass."

"About time," I groaned. "Let's hope there are animals too — I'll crack up if I have to eat another lizard or bug."

"What do you think those twelve-legged … insects were that we ate yesterday?" Harkat asked.

"I've no idea, but I won't be touching them again — my stomach was in bits all night!"

Harkat chuckled. "They didn't bother me. Sometimes it helps to have no … taste buds, and a stomach capable of digesting … almost anything."

Harkat pulled his mask up over his mouth and breathed through it in silence, studying the land ahead. Harkat had spent a lot of time testing the air, and didn't think it was poisonous to him – it was slightly different to the air on Earth, more acidic – but he kept his mask on anyway, to be safe. I'd coughed a lot for the first few days, but I was OK now — my hardened lungs had adapted to the bitter air.

"Decided where we are yet?" I asked after a while. That was our favourite topic of conversation. We'd narrowed the possibilities down to four options. Mr Tiny had somehow sent us back into the past. He'd transported us to some far-off world in our own universe. He'd slipped us into an alternate reality. Or this was an illusion, and our bodies were lying in a field in the real world, while Mr Tiny fed this dream scene into our imaginations.

"I believed in the … illusion theory at first," Harkat said, lowering his mask. "But the more I consider it, the less … certain I am. If Mr Tiny was making this world up, I think … he'd make it more exciting and colourful. It's quite drab."

"It's early days," I grunted. "This is probably just to warm us up."

"It certainly warmed *you* up," Harkat grinned, nodding at my tan.

I returned his smile, then stared up at the sun. "Another three or four hours till nightfall," I guessed. "It's a shame neither of us knows more about star systems, or we might be able to tell where we were by the stars."

"It's a bigger shame that we … don't have weapons," Harkat noted. He stood and studied the land in front of us again. "How will we defend ourselves against the … panther without weapons?"

"Something will turn up," I reassured him. "Mr Tiny wouldn't throw us in out of our depth, not this early on — it'd spoil his fun if we perished quickly."

"That's not very comforting," Harkat said. "The idea that we're being kept alive ... only to die horribly later, for Mr Tiny's benefit ... doesn't fill me with joy."

"Me neither," I agreed. "But at least it gives us hope."

On that uncertain note, the conversation drew to a close, and after a short rest we filled our meagre lizard-skin pouches with water and marched on through the wasteland, which grew more lush — but no less alien — the further we progressed.

# CHAPTER SIX

A WEEK after leaving the desert behind, we entered a jungle of thick cactus plants, long snaking vines, and stunted, twisted trees. Very few leaves grew on the trees. Those that did were long and thin, a dull orange colour, grouped near the tops of the trees.

We'd come across traces of animals – droppings, bones, hair – but didn't see any until we entered the jungle. There we found a curious mix of familiar yet strange creatures. Most of the animals were similar to those of Earth – deer, squirrels, monkeys – but different, usually in size or colouring. Some of the differences weren't so readily apparent — we captured a squirrel one day, which turned out to have an extra set of sharp teeth when we examined it, and surprisingly long claws.

We'd picked up dagger-shaped stones during the course of our trek, which we'd sharpened into knives. We now made more weapons out of thick sticks and bones of larger animals. They wouldn't be much use against a panther, but they helped us frighten off the small yellow monkeys which jumped from trees on to the heads of their victims, blinded them with their claws and teeth, then finished them off as they stumbled around.

"I never heard of monkeys like that," I remarked one morning as we watched a group of the simians bring down and devour a huge boar-like animal.

"Me neither," Harkat said.

As we watched, the monkeys paused and sniffed the air suspiciously. One ran to a thick bush and screeched threateningly. There was a deep grunt from within the bush, then a larger monkey – like a baboon, only an odd red colour – stepped out and shook a long arm at the others. The yellow monkeys bared their teeth, hissed and threw twigs and small pebbles at the newcomer, but the baboon ignored them and advanced. The smaller monkeys retreated, leaving the baboon to finish off the boar.

"I guess size matters," I muttered wryly, then Harkat and I slipped away and left the baboon to feed in peace.

The next night, while Harkat slept – his nightmares had stopped since coming to this new world – and I stood guard, there was a loud, fierce roar from somewhere ahead of us. The night was usually filled with the nonstop sounds of insects and other nocturnal creatures, but at the roar all noise ceased. There was total silence – once the echoes of the roar subsided – for at least five minutes.

Harkat slept through the roar. He was normally a light sleeper, but the air here agreed with him and he'd been dozing more deeply. I told him about it in the morning.

"You think it was ... our panther?" he asked.

"It was definitely a big cat," I said. "It might have been a lion or tiger, but my money's on the black panther."

"Panthers are usually very quiet," Harkat said. "But I guess they could be ... different here. If this is his territory, he should come by ... this way soon. Panthers are on constant patrol. We must prepare." During his time in Vampire Mountain, when he'd been working for Seba Nile, Harkat had spoken with several vampires who'd hunted or fought with lions and leopards, so he knew quite a lot about them. "We must dig a pit to ... lure it into, catch and truss a deer, and also find some ... porcupines."

"Porcupines?" I asked.

"Their quills can stick in the panther's ... paws, snout and mouth. They might slow it down or ... distract it."

"We're going to need more than porcupine quills to kill a panther," I noted.

"With luck, we'll startle it when ... it comes to feed on the deer. We can jump out and frighten it into ... the pit. Hopefully it will die there."

"And if it doesn't?" I asked.

Harkat grinned edgily. "We're in trouble. Black panthers are really leopards, and leopards are ... the worst of the big cats. They're fast, strong, savage and ... great climbers. We won't be able to outrun it or ... climb higher than it."

"So if plan A fails, there's no plan B?"

"No." Harkat chuckled dryly. "It'll be straight to plan P
— *Panic!*"

We found a clearing with a thick bush at one end where we'd
be able to hide. We spent the morning digging a deep pit with
our hands and the rough tools we'd fashioned from branches
and bones. When the pit was done, we harvested a couple of
dozen thick branches and sharpened the tips, creating stakes
that we were going to place in the base of the pit.

As we were climbing into the pit to plant the stakes, I
stopped at the edge and started to tremble — remembering
another pit that had been filled with stakes, and the friend I'd
lost there.

"What's wrong?" Harkat asked. Before I could answer, he
read it in my eyes. "Oh," he sighed. "Mr Crepsley."

"Isn't there any other way to kill it?" I groaned.

"Not without proper equipment." Harkat took my stakes
from me and smiled encouragingly. "Go hunt for porcupines.
I'll handle this … end of the operation."

Nodding gratefully, I left Harkat to plant the stakes and
went looking for porcupines or anything else to use against
the panther. I hadn't thought much about Mr Crepsley lately
– this harsh world had demanded my full attention – but the
pit brought it all crashing back. Again I saw him drop and
heard his screams as he died. I wanted to leave the pit and
panther, but that wasn't an option. We had to kill the predator
to learn where to go next. So I quashed thoughts of Mr
Crepsley as best I could and immersed myself in work.

I picked some of the sturdier cacti to use as missiles against the black panther, and made mud-balls using leaves and fresh mud from a nearby stream — I hoped the mud might temporarily blind the panther. I searched hard for porcupines, but if any were in the vicinity, they were keeping an ultra low profile. I had to report back quill-less to Harkat in the afternoon.

"Never mind," he said, sitting by the edge of the completed pit. "Let's create a cover for this and ... catch a deer. After that we're in the lap ... of the gods."

We built a thin cover for the pit out of long twigs and leaves, laid it over the hole and went hunting. The deer here were shorter than those on Earth, with longer heads. They couldn't run as fast as their Earth counterparts, but were still pretty swift. It took a while to track down a lame straggler and bring it back alive. It was dusk by the time we tied it to a stake close to the pit, and we were both tired after our long, taxing day.

"What happens if the panther attacks during the night?" I asked, sheltering under a skin I'd sliced from a deer with a small stone scraper.

"Why do you always have to anticipate ... the worst?" Harkat grumbled.

"Somebody has to," I laughed. "Will it be plan P time?"

"No," Harkat sighed. "If he comes in the dark, it's ... KYAG time."

"KYAG?" I echoed.

"Kiss Your Ass Goodbye!"

\* \* \*

62

There was no sign of the panther that night, though we both heard deep-throated growls, closer than the roars of the night before. As soon as dawn broke, we ate a hasty breakfast — berries we'd picked after seeing monkeys eat them — and positioned ourselves in the thick covering bush opposite the staked deer and pit. If all went according to plan, the panther would attack the deer. With luck it'd come at it from the far side of the pit and fall in. If not, we'd leap up whilst it was dragging off the deer and hopefully force it backwards to its doom. Not the most elaborate plan in the world, but it would have to do.

We said nothing as the minutes turned to hours, silently waiting for the panther. My mouth was dry and I sipped frequently from the squirrel skin beakers (we'd replaced the lizard-skin containers) by my side, though only small amounts — to cut out too many toilet trips.

About an hour after midday I laid a hand on Harkat's grey arm and squeezed warningly — I'd seen something long and black through the trees. Both of us stared hard. As we did, I saw the tip of a whiskered nose stick out from around a tree and sniff the air testingly — the panther! I kept my mouth closed, willing the panther to advance, but after a few hesitant seconds it turned and padded away into the gloom of the jungle.

Harkat and I looked questioningly at one another. "It must have smelt us," I whispered.

"Or sensed something wrong," Harkat whispered back. Lifting his head slightly, he studied the grazing deer by the pit, then jerked a thumb backwards. "Let's get further away. I think it will return. If we aren't here, it might be … tempted to attack."

"We won't have a clear view if we withdraw any further," I noted.

"I know," Harkat said, "but we've no choice. It knew something was wrong. If we stay here, it'll also know when … it returns, and won't come any closer."

I followed Harkat as he wriggled further back into the bush, not stopping until we were almost at the end of the briars and vines. From here we could only vaguely see the deer.

An hour passed. Two. I was beginning to abandon hope that the panther would return, when the sound of deep breathing drifted towards us from the clearing. I caught flashes of the deer jumping around, straining to break free of its rope. Something growled throatily — the panther. Even more promising — the growls were coming from the far side of the pit. If the panther attacked the deer from there, it would fall straight into our trap!

Harkat and I lay motionless, barely breathing. We heard twigs snap as the panther closed in on the deer, not masking its sounds any longer. Then there was a loud snapping sound as a heavy body crashed through the covering over the pit and landed heavily on the stakes. There was a ferocious howl and I had to cover my ears with my hands. That was followed by silence, disturbed only by the pounding of the deer's hooves on the soil as it leapt around by the edge of the pit.

Harkat slowly got to his feet and stared over the bush at the open pit. I stood and stared with him. We glanced at each other and I said uncertainly, "It worked."

"You sound like you didn't … expect it to," Harkat grinned.

"I didn't," I laughed, and started towards the pit.

"Careful," Harkat warned me, hefting a knobbly, heavy wooden club. "It could still be alive. There's nothing more dangerous than … a wounded animal."

"It'd be howling with pain if it was alive," I said.

"Probably," Harkat nodded, "but let's not take any … needless risks." Stepping in front of me, he moved off to the left and signalled me to go right. Raising a knife-like piece of bone, I circled away from Harkat, then we slowly closed on the pit from opposite directions. As we got nearer, we each drew one of the small cacti we'd tied to our waists – we also had mud-balls strapped on – to toss like grenades if the panther was still alive.

Harkat came within sight of the pit before I did and stopped, confused. As I got closer, I saw what had bewildered him. I also drew to a halt, not sure what to make of it. A body lay impaled on the stakes, blood dripping from its many puncture wounds. But it wasn't the body of a panther — it was a red baboon.

"I don't understand," I muttered. "Monkeys can't make the kind of growling or howling sounds we heard."

"But how did…" Harkat stopped and fear flashed into his eyes. "The monkey's throat!" he gasped. "It's been ripped open! The panther must—"

He got no further. Even as I was leaping to the same conclusion – the panther had killed the baboon and dropped it into the pit to fool us! – there was a blur of movement in the upper branches of the tree closest to me. Whirling, I caught a very brief glimpse of a long, thick, pure black object flying through the air with outstretched claws and gaping jaws — then the panther was upon me, roaring triumphantly as it dragged me to the ground for the kill!

# CHAPTER SEVEN

THE ROAR was critical. If the panther had clamped its fangs clean around my throat, I wouldn't have stood a chance. But the animal was excited – probably by having outsmarted us – and tossed its head, growling savagely as we rolled over and came to a stop with the powerful beast on top of me.

As it roared, Harkat reacted with cool speed and launched a cactus missile. It could have bounced off the animal's head or shoulders, but the luck of the vampires was with us, and the cactus sailed clean between the panther's fearsome jaws.

The panther instantly lost interest in me and lurched aside, spitting and scratching at the cactus stuck in its mouth. I crawled away, panting, scrabbling for the knife I'd dropped. Harkat leapt over me as my fingers closed around the handle of the bone, and brought his club down upon the head of the panther.

If the club had been made of tougher material, Harkat would have killed the panther — he could do immense damage with most axes or clubs. But the wood he'd carved it from proved unworthy of the task, and the club smashed in half as it cracked over the panther's hard skull.

The panther howled with pain and rage, and turned on Harkat, spitting spines, its yellow teeth reflecting the gleam of the afternoon sun. It swiped at his squat grey head and opened up a deep gash down the left side of his face. Harkat fell backwards from the force of the blow and the panther leapt after him.

I didn't have time to get up and lunge after the panther — it would be on Harkat before I crossed the space between us — so I sent my knife flying through the air at it. The bone deflected harmlessly off the creature's powerful flanks, but it distracted the beast and its head snapped around. Harkat used the moment to grab a couple of the mud-balls hanging from his blue robes. When the panther faced him again, Harkat let it have the mud-balls between the eyes.

The panther squealed and turned a sharp ninety degrees away from Harkat. It scraped at its eyes with its left paw, wiping the mud away. As it was doing that, Harkat grabbed the lower half of his broken club and jammed the splintered end into the panther's ribcage. The club penetrated the panther's body, but only slightly, drawing blood but not puncturing the panther's lungs.

That was too much for the panther — it went berserk. Even though it couldn't see properly, it threw itself at Harkat, hissing and spitting, swiping with its deadly claws. Harkat ducked out of the way, but the panther's claws snagged on the hem of his robes. Before he could free himself, the predator was on him, working blindly, its teeth gnashing together in search of Harkat's face.

Harkat wrapped his arms tight around the panther and squeezed, trying to snap its ribs or suffocate it. While he did that, I leapt on the panther's back and raked at its nose and eyes with another cactus head. The panther caught the cactus with its teeth and ripped it clear of my grasp — almost taking my right thumb with it!

"Get off!" Harkat wheezed as I clung to the panther's heaving shoulders and scrabbled for another cactus.

"I think I can–" I started to shout.

"*Off!*" Harkat roared.

There was no arguing with a cry like that. I let go of the panther and slumped to the ground. As I did, Harkat locked his hands even tighter together and spun, looking for the pit through the green blood streaming into his wide left eye. Finding it, he clutched the struggling panther close to his chest, stumbled towards the pit — and threw himself in!

"Harkat!" I screamed, reaching out automatically, as though I could grab and save him. The picture of Mr Crepsley falling into the pit of stakes in the Cavern of Retribution flashed through my head, and my insides turned to lead.

There was an ugly thud and an agonizing screech as the panther was impaled on the stakes. No sound came from

Harkat, which made me think he'd landed beneath the panther and died instantly.

"*No!*" I moaned, picking myself up and hobbling towards the edge of the pit. I was so worried about Harkat that I almost toppled into the pit myself! As I stood on the edge, arms swinging wildly to correct my balance, there was a low groan and I saw Harkat's head turn. He'd landed on top of the panther — he was alive!

"Harkat!" I shouted again, joyously this time.

"Help … me … up," he gasped. The panther's limbs were still twitching, but they no longer presented a threat — it was nearing the final stages of its death throes and wouldn't have had the strength to kill Harkat even if it wished to.

Lying on my stomach, I reached down into the pit and offered Harkat my hand, but he couldn't reach. He was lying flat on the panther, and although the creature – and the baboon underneath – had taken the worst of the stakes, several had pierced Harkat, a few in his legs, a couple in his stomach and chest, and one through the flesh of his upper left arm. The wounds to his legs and body didn't look too serious. The one through his arm was the problem — he was stuck on the stake and couldn't raise his right hand high enough to clutch mine.

"Wait there," I said, looking around for something to lower to him.

"As if … I could go … anywhere!" I heard him mutter sarcastically.

We didn't have any rope, but there were plenty of strong vines growing nearby. Hurrying to the nearest, I sawed at it with my fingernails, cutting off a two metre length. I grabbed it tightly near both ends and tugged sharply to test it. The vine didn't snap under the strain, so I returned to the pit and fed down one end to Harkat. The Little Person grabbed it with his free right hand, waited until I'd got a good grip on my end, then yanked his left arm free of the stake. He gasped tightly as his flesh slid off the piercing wood. Grasping the vine tight, he swung his feet on to the wall of the pit and walked up it, pulling on the vine at the same time.

Harkat was almost at the top when his feet slipped. As his legs dropped, I realized his falling weight would drag us both down if I held on to the rope. I released it with snake-like speed, collapsed to my stomach and clutched for Harkat's hands.

I missed his hands, but my fingers closed on the left sleeve of his blue robes. There was a terrifying ripping sound and I thought I'd lost him, but the material held, and after a few dangerous, dangling seconds I was able to haul the Little Person up out of the pit.

Rolling on to his back, Harkat stared up at the sky, his grey, stitched-together face looking even more like a corpse's than usual. I tried to get up, but my legs were trembling, so I flopped beside him and the two of us lay there in silence, breathing heavily, marvelling inwardly at the fact that we were still alive.

# CHAPTER EIGHT

I PATCHED Harkat up as best I could, cleaning out his wounds with water from the stream, slicing my jumper into strips to use as bandages. If I'd been a full-vampire I could have used my spit to close his cuts, but as a half-vampire I lacked that ability.

The wounds to his face — where the panther had clawed him — should have been stitched, but neither of us had any thread or needles. I suggested improvising and using a small bone and animal hair, but Harkat waved the idea away. "I've enough stitches," he grinned. "Let it heal as it likes. I can't get any uglier ... than I already am."

"That's true," I agreed, and laughed as he swatted me round the back of my head. I swiftly grew serious again. "If infection sets in..."

"Looking on the bright side as usual," he groaned, then shrugged. "If it sets in, I'm finished — no ... hospitals here. Let's not worry ... about it."

I helped Harkat to his feet and we returned to the edge of the pit to gaze down at the panther. Harkat was limping worse than normal – he'd always had a slight limp in his left leg – but he said he wasn't in much pain. The panther was a metre and a half in length and thickly built. As we stared at it, I could hardly believe we'd bested it in the fight. Not for the first time in my life, I got the feeling that if vampire gods existed, they were keeping a close watch on me and lending a helping hand whenever I strayed out of my depth.

"You know what worries me … the most?" Harkat asked after a while. "Mr Tiny said the panther was … the *least* of our worries. That means there's worse ahead!"

"Now who's being pessimistic?" I snorted. "Want me to go down and get the panther out?"

"Let's wait until morning," Harkat said. "We'll build a good fire, eat, rest … and drag the panther … up tomorrow."

That sounded good to me, so while Harkat made a fire – using flinty stones to create sparks – I butchered the deer and set about carving it up. Once upon a time I might have let the deer go, but vampires are predators. We hunt and kill without remorse, the same as any other animal of the wilds.

The meat, when we cooked it, was tough, stringy and unappealing, but we ate ravenously, both aware of how fortunate we were not to *be* the main course that night.

I climbed down into the pit in the morning and prised the panther off the stakes. Leaving the baboon where it lay I passed the panther's carcass up to Harkat. It wasn't as easy as it sounds – the panther was very heavy – but we were stronger than humans, so it wasn't one of our harder tasks.

We studied the panther's gleaming black corpse, wondering how it would tell us where to go. "Maybe we have to slice it open," I suggested. "There might be a box or canister inside."

"Worth trying," Harkat agreed, and rolled the panther over on its back, presenting us with its smooth, soft stomach.

"Wait!" I shouted as Harkat prepared to make the first cut. The hair on the panther's underside wasn't quite as dark as elsewhere. I could see the stretched skin of its stomach — and there was something drawn on it! I searched among our makeshift knives for one with a long, straight edge, then scraped away some of the hairs on the dead panther's stomach. Thin raised lines were revealed.

"That's just scar tissue," Harkat said.

"No," I disagreed. "Look at the circular shapes and the way they spread out. They've been carved deliberately. Help me scrape the entire stomach clear."

It didn't take long to shave the panther and reveal a detailed map. It must have been gouged into the panther's stomach many years ago, maybe when it was a cub. There was a small X at the extreme right of the map, which seemed to indicate our current position. Towards the left an area was circled, and something had been written within the circle.

"Go to the home of the world's largest toad," I read aloud. "Grab the gelatinous globes."

That's all it said. We read it a few more times, then shared a puzzled look. "Any idea what 'gelatinous' means?" Harkat asked.

"I think it's got something to do with jelly," I answered uncertainly.

"So we've got to find the world's ... largest toad, and grab globes made out of jelly?" Harkat sounded dubious.

"This is Mr Tiny we're dealing with," I reminded him. "He makes jokes out of everything. I think our best bet's simply to follow the map from here to the circle and worry about the rest once we get there."

Harkat nodded, then set about the panther's stomach with a sharp stone knife, cutting free the map. "Here," I stopped him. "Let me. I've got nimbler fingers."

As I carefully cut around the edges of the map and sliced the panther's flesh away from its insides, Harkat strolled around the dead beast, mulling something over. As I peeled the map free of the panther and wiped the inside of it clean on a patch of grass, Harkat stopped. "Do you recall Mr Tiny saying he'd ... thrown in a clue to my identity?" he asked.

I cast my thoughts back. "Yes. Maybe that's what the message within the circle means."

"I doubt it," Harkat replied. "Whoever I was before I died, I'm pretty ... sure I wasn't a toad!"

"Maybe you're a frog prince," I giggled.

"Ha bloody ha," Harkat said. "I'm sure the writing's got nothing ... to do with me. There must be something else."

I studied the dead panther. "If you want to root around in its guts, feel free," I told Harkat. "I'm content with the map."

Harkat crouched beside me and flexed his stubby grey fingers, intent on ripping out the panther's insides. I shifted away, not wanting to be part of the messy task. As I did, my eyes flicked to the panther's mouth. Its lips were curled up over its teeth in a frozen death snarl. I laid a hand on Harkat's left arm and said softly, "Look."

When Harkat saw what I was pointing at, he reached over to the panther's mouth and prised its stiff lips entirely clear of its fangs. There were small black letters etched into most of the creature's teeth — an A, a K, an M and others. "There!" Harkat grunted with excitement. "That must be it."

"I'll hold the head up," I said, "so that you can read all the—"

But before I'd finished, Harkat had grasped one of the panther's largest teeth with his fingers and attacked its gums with a knife held in his right. I saw that he was fixed on extracting all the teeth, so I left him to it while he hacked them loose.

When Harkat was done, he took the teeth to the stream and washed them clean of blood. When he returned, he scattered the teeth on the ground and we bent over them to try and decipher the mystery. There were eleven teeth in all, host to a variety of letters. I arranged them alphabetically so that we could see exactly what we had. There were two A's, followed by a single D, H, K, L, M, R, S, T and U.

"We must be able to make a ... message out of them," Harkat said.

"Eleven letters," I mused. "It can't be a very long message. Let's see what we can come up with." I shifted the letters around until I got three words – ASK MUD RAT – with two letters left over, H and L.

Harkat tried and got SLAM DARK HUT.

As I was juggling them around again, Harkat groaned, pushed me aside and began rearranging the teeth purposefully. "Have you worked it out?" I asked, slightly disappointed that he'd beaten me to the punch.

"Yes," he said, "but it's not a clue — just Mr Tiny ... being smug." He finished laying out the teeth and waved at them bitterly — HARKAT MULDS.

"What's the point of that?" I grumbled. "That's a waste of time."

"Mr Tiny loves playing with time," Harkat sighed, then wrapped the teeth in a piece of cloth and tucked them away inside his robes.

"What are you hanging on to them for?" I asked.

"They're sharp," Harkat said. "They might come in useful." He stood and walked over to where the map was drying in the sun. "Will we be able to use this?" he asked, studying the lines and squiggles.

"If it's accurate," I replied.

"Then let's get going," Harkat said, rolling the map up and sticking it inside his robes along with the teeth. "I'm anxious to meet the world's ... largest toad." He looked at me and grinned. "And to see if there's any ... family resemblance."

Laughing, we broke camp quickly and set off through the trees, eager to leave behind the clouds of flies and insects gathering to feast on the corpse of the defeated lord of the jungle.

# CHAPTER NINE

ABOUT THREE weeks later, we came to the edge of a huge swamp — the area marked on the map by the circle. It had been a relatively easy trek. The map had been plainly drawn and was simple to follow. Though the terrain was tricky to negotiate — lots of wiry bushes to cut through — it didn't present any life-threatening problems. Harkat's wounds had healed without complications but he was left with three very noticeable scars on the left side of his face — almost as if he'd been marked by an especially eager vampaneze!

A foul smell of putrid water and rotting plants emanated from the swamp. The air was thick with flying insects. As we stood and watched, we spotted a couple of water snakes attack, kill and devour a large rat with four yellow eyes.

"I don't like the look of this," I muttered.

"You haven't seen the worst yet," Harkat said, pointing to a small island off to our left, jutting out of the waters of the swamp. I couldn't see what he was talking about at first – the island was bare except for three large logs – but then one of the "logs" moved.

"Alligators!" I hissed.

"Very bad news for *you*," Harkat said.

"Why me in particular?" I asked.

"*I* wrestled the panther," he grinned. "The alligators are *yours*."

"You've a warped sense of humour, Mulds," I growled, then stepped back from the edge of the swamp. "Let's circle around and try to find the toad."

"You know it's not going to be ... on the outskirts," Harkat said. "We'll have to wade in."

"I know," I sighed, "but let's at least try and find an entry spot that isn't guarded by alligators. We won't get very far if that lot get a whiff of us."

We walked for hours along the rim of the swamp, without sight or sound of a toad, though we did find lots of small brown frogs. We saw plenty more snakes and alligators too. Finally we came to a section with no visible predators. The water was shallow and slightly less pungent than elsewhere. It was as good a place as any to wet our toes.

"I wish I had Mr Tiny's ... Wellington boots," Harkat grumbled, knotting the hem of his blue robes above his knees.

"Me too," I sighed, rolling up the bottoms of my jeans. I paused as I was about to set foot in the water. "I just thought of something. This stretch of swamp could be full of piranha — that might be why there are no alligators or snakes!"

Harkat stared at me with something close to loathing in his round green eyes. "Why can't you keep stupid thoughts ... like that to yourself?" he snapped.

"I'm serious," I insisted. I got down on my hands and knees and peered into the still waters of the swamp, but it was too cloudy to see anything.

"I think piranha only attack when ... they scent blood," Harkat said. "If there are piranha, we should ... be OK as long as we don't cut ourselves."

"It's times like these that I really hate Mr Tiny," I groaned. But since there was nothing else for it, I stepped into the swamp. I paused, ready to leap out at the first hint of a bite, then waded ahead cautiously, Harkat following close behind.

A few hours later, as dusk was lengthening, we found an uninhabited island. Harkat and I hauled ourselves out of the swampy water and collapsed with exhaustion. We then slept, me sheltered beneath the deer blanket I'd been using these last few weeks, Harkat beneath the fleshy map we'd stripped from the black panther's stomach. But we didn't sleep deeply. The swamp was alive with noises — insects, frogs and the occasional unidentifiable splash. We were bleary-eyed and shivering when we rose the following morning.

One good thing about the filthy swamp was that the water level remained fairly low. Every so often we'd hit a dip and one or both of us would slip and disappear under the murky water, only to bob up spluttering and cursing moments later. But most of the time the water didn't reach higher than our thighs. Another bonus was that although the swamp was teeming with insects and leeches, they didn't bother us — our skin was obviously too tough and our blood off-putting.

We avoided the alligators, circling far around them whenever we saw one. Although we were attacked several times by snakes, we were too quick and strong for them. But we had to remain on constant alert — one slip could be the end of us.

"No piranha so far," Harkat noted as we rested. We'd been working our way through a long swath of tall reeds, full of irritating sticky seeds which had stuck to my hair and clothes.

"In cases like this, I'm delighted to be proved wrong," I said.

"We could spend months … searching for this toad," Harkat commented.

"I don't think it'll take that long," I said. "By the law of averages, it should take ages to locate anything specific in a swamp this size. But Mr Tiny has a way of fiddling with laws. He wants us to find the toad, so I'm sure we will."

"If that's the case," Harkat mused, "maybe we should just … do nothing and wait for the toad to … come to us."

"It doesn't work that way," I said. "Mr Tiny's set this up, but we have to sweat to make it happen. If we sat on the edge of the swamp – or if we hadn't marched west when he said – we'd lose touch with the game and would no longer be under his influence — meaning he couldn't stack the odds in our favour."

Harkat studied me curiously. "You've been thinking about this … a lot," he remarked.

"Not much else to do in this godsforsaken world," I laughed.

Flicking off the last of the seeds, we rested a few more minutes, then set off, silent and grim-faced, wading through the murky waters, our eyes peeled for predators as we moved ever further into the heart of the swamp.

As the sun was setting, a deep-throated croaking noise drifted to us from the middle of an island covered by thick bushes and gnarly trees. We knew at once that it was our toad, just as we'd instantly recognized the panther by its roar. Wading up to the rim of the island, we paused to consider our options.

"The sun will be gone in a few … minutes," Harkat said. "Perhaps we should wait for … morning."

"But the moon will be almost full tonight," I pointed out. "This might be as good a time as any to act — bright enough for us to see, but dark enough for us to hide."

Harkat looked at me quizzically. "You sound as though you … fear this toad."

"Remember Evanna's frogs?" I asked, referring to a group of frogs that guarded the witch's home. They had sacs of poison along the sides of their tongues — it was deadly if it got into your bloodstream. "I know this is a toad, not a frog, but we'd be fools to take it for granted."

"OK," Harkat said. "We'll go in when the moon's up. If we don't like the … look of it, we can return tomorrow."

We crouched on the edge of the island while the moon rose and illuminated the night sky. Then, drawing our weapons – a knife for me, a spear for Harkat – we pushed through the damp overhanging fronds and crept slowly past the various trees and plants. After several minutes we came to a clearing at the centre of the island, where we paused under cover of a bush and gawped at the spectacular sight ahead.

A wide moat ran around a curved mound of mud and reeds. To the left and right of the moat, alligators lay in wait, four or five on each side. On the mound in the middle lay the toad — and it was a *monster*! Two metres long, with a huge, knobbly body, an immense head with bulging eyes, and an enormous mouth. Its skin was a dark, crinkled, greeny brown colour. It was pockmarked all over, and out of the holes oozed some sort of slimy yellow pus. Thick black leeches slowly slid up and down its hide, like mobile beauty spots, feeding on the pus.

As we stared incredulously at the giant toad, a crow-like bird flew by overhead. The toad's head lifted slightly, then its mouth snapped open and its tongue shot out, impossibly long and thick. It snatched the bird from the air. There was a squawk and a flurried flapping of wings. Then the crow disappeared and the toad's jaw moved up and down as it swallowed the hapless bird.

I was so taken aback by the toad's appearance that I didn't notice the small clear balls surrounding it. It was only when Harkat tapped my arm and pointed that I realized the toad was sitting on what must be the 'gelatinous globes'. We'd have to cross the moat and sneak the globes out from underneath it!

Withdrawing, we huddled in the shadows of the bushes and trees to discuss our next move. "Know what we need?" I whispered to Harkat.

"What?"

"The world's biggest jam jar."

Harkat groaned. "Be serious," he chastized me. "How are we going to get the ... globes without that thing taking our heads off?"

"We'll have to sneak up from behind and hope it doesn't notice," I said. "I was watching its tongue when it struck the crow. I didn't spot any poison sacs along the sides."

"What about the alligators?" Harkat asked. "Are they waiting to attack the toad?"

"No," I said. "I think they're protecting it or living in harmony with it, like the leeches."

"I never heard of alligators doing that," Harkat noted sceptically.

"And *I* never heard of a toad bigger than a cow," I retorted. "Who knows how this mad world functions? Maybe all the toads are that size."

The best we could do would be to create a distraction, nip in, grab the globes, and get out again — fast! Retreating to the edge of the island, we waded through the swamp in search of something we could use to distract the alligators. We killed a couple of large water rats, and captured three live creatures unlike anything we'd seen before. They were shaped like turtles, except with see-through, soft shells and nine powerful fins. They were harmless — speed was their single natural defence. We only caught them when they became entangled in weeds on a mud bank as we were chasing them.

Returning to the island, we crept up on the monstrous toad at the centre and paused in the bushes. "I've been thinking," Harkat whispered. "It makes more sense for only … one of us to move on the toad. The other should hold on to the … rats and turtles, and throw them to … the alligators to provide cover."

"That sounds sensible," I agreed. "Any thoughts on who should go in?"

I expected Harkat to volunteer, but he smiled sheepishly and said, "I think *you* should go."

"Oh?" I replied, momentarily thrown.

"You're faster than me," Harkat said. "You stand a better chance of … making it back alive. Of course, if you … don't want to…"

"Don't be stupid," I grunted. "I'll do it. Just make sure you keep those 'gators occupied."

"I'll do my best," Harkat said, then slipped off to the left, to find the ideal position to launch the rats and turtle-like creatures.

I nudged my way around to the rear of the toad, so I could sneak up on it without being seen, and wriggled down to the edge of the moat. There was a stick lying nearby which I stuck into the water, testing its depth. It didn't seem deep. I was sure I could wade the six or seven metres towards the toad's base.

There was a rustling motion off to my left and one of the turtle creatures went zooming through the air, landing amidst the alligators on the far right side. One of the dead rats was quickly hurled among the other alligators on the left of the moat. As soon as the alligators began snapping at each other and fighting for the morsels, I lowered myself into the cold, clammy water. It was filled with soggy twigs, dead insects and slime from the toad's sores. I ignored the disgusting mess and waded across to where the toad was squatting, its eyes fixed on the bickering alligators.

There were several jelly-like globes near the edge of the toad's perch. I picked up a couple, meaning to stuff them inside my shirt, but their soft shells were broken. They lost their shape and a sticky clear fluid oozed out of them.

Glancing up, I saw another of the turtles flying through the air, followed by the second dead rat. That meant Harkat only had one of the turtles held in reserve. I had to act fast. Slithering forward on to the mound, I reached for the shiny globes lying closest to the giant toad. Most were covered with pus. It was warm, with the texture of vomit, and the stench made me gag. Holding my breath, I wiped the pus away and found a globe that wasn't broken. I sifted through the shells and found another, then another. The globes were different sizes, some only five or six centimetres in diameter, some twenty centimetres. I packed loads of the globes inside my shirt, working quickly. I'd just about gathered enough when the toad's head turned and I found myself on the end of its fierce, bulging gaze.

I reacted swiftly and spun away, stumbling back towards the island across the moat. As I lunged to safety, the toad unleashed its tongue and struck me hard on my right shoulder, knocking me flat. I came up gasping, spitting out water and bits of jelly and pus. The toad lashed me with its tongue again, connected with the top of my head and sent me flying a second time. As I came up out of the water, dazed, I caught sight of several objects sliding into the moat beyond the mound. I lost all interest in the toad and its tongue. I had a far greater threat to worry about. The alligators had finished with the scraps Harkat had thrown them. Now they were coming after a fresh snack — *me!*

# CHAPTER TEN

TURNING MY back on the alligators, I scrambled for the bank. I might have made it if the toad hadn't struck me again with its tongue, this time whipping the tip of it around my throat and spinning me back towards it. The toad hadn't enough power to pull me all the way to the mound, but I landed close to it. As I sprang to my feet, gasping for breath, I spotted the first of the onrushing alligators and knew I'd never make it to the bank in time.

Standing my ground, I prepared to meet the alligator's challenge. My aim was to clamp its jaws shut and keep them closed — it couldn't do much damage with its tiny front claws. But even assuming I could do that, I'd no way of dealing with the rest of the pack, which were coming fast on the lead alligator's tail.

I glimpsed Harkat splashing into the water, rushing to my aid, but the fight would be long over by the time he reached me. The first alligator homed in on me, eyes glinting cruelly, snout lifting as it bared its fangs – so many! so long! so sharp! – to crush me. I drew my hands apart and started bringing them together...

... when, on the bank to my right, a figure appeared and screeched something unintelligible while waving its arms high in the air.

There was a lightning-bright flash in the sky overhead. I instinctively covered my eyes with my hands. When I removed them a few seconds later, I saw that the alligator had missed me and run aground on the bank. The other alligators were all in a muddle, swimming around in circles and crashing into one another. On the mound, the toad had lowered its head and was croaking deeply, paying no attention to me.

I gazed from the alligators to Harkat – he'd stopped in confusion – then at the figure on the bank. As it lowered its arms, I saw that it was a person — a woman! And as she stepped forward, out of the shadows of the trees, revealing her long straggly hair and body-wrapping ropes, I recognized her.

"*Evanna?*" I roared in disbelief.

"That was pretty finely timed, even by my standards," the witch grunted, coming to a halt at the edge of the moat.

"*Evanna?*" Harkat cried.

"Is there an echo?" the witch sniffed, then glanced around at the alligators and toad. "I've cast a temporary blinding spell on the creatures, but it won't last long. If you value your lives, get out of there, and quick!"

"But how ... what ... where..." I stuttered.

"Let's talk about it on ... dry land," Harkat said, crossing over to join me, carefully skirting the thrashing alligators. "Did you get the globes?"

"Yes," I said, pulling one out from within my shirt. "But how did she—"

"Later!" Harkat snapped, pushing me towards safety.

Suppressing my questions, I stumbled to the bank and crawled out of the mucky water of the moat. Evanna caught me by the back of my shirt and hauled me to my feet, then grabbed Harkat's robes and pulled him up too. "Come on," she said, retreating. "We'd best not be here when their sight clears. That toad has a nasty temper and might bound after us."

Harkat and I paused to consider what would happen if a toad that size leapt upon us. Then we hurried after the departing witch as fast as our weary legs could carry us.

Evanna had established her camp on a grassy isle a few hundred metres from the island of the toad. A fire was burning when we crawled out of the swamp, a vegetable stew bubbling in a pot above it. Replacement clothes were waiting for us, blue robes for Harkat, dark brown trousers and a shirt for me.

"Get out of those wet rags, get dry, and get dressed," Evanna ordered, going to check on the stew.

Harkat and I stared from the witch, to the fire, to the clothes.

"This probably sounds like a stupid question," I said, "but have you been expecting us?"

"Of course," Evanna said. "I've been here for the past week. I guessed you wouldn't arrive that soon, but I didn't want to risk missing you."

"How did you know we ... were coming?" Harkat asked.

"Please," Evanna sighed. "You know of my magical powers and my ability to predict future events. Don't trouble me with unnecessary questions."

"So tell us why you're here," I encouraged her. "And why you rescued us. As I recall, you've always said you couldn't get involved in our battles."

"Not in your fight with the vampaneze," Evanna said. "When it comes to alligators and toads, I have a free hand. Now why don't you change out of your damp clothes and eat some of this delicious stew before you pester me with more of your dratted questions?"

Since it was uncomfortable standing there wet and hungry, we did as the witch advised. After a quick meal, as we were licking our fingers clean, I asked Evanna if she could tell us where we were. "No," she said.

"Could you transport Darren ... back home?" Harkat asked.

"I'm going nowhere!" I objected immediately.

"You just narrowly survived being ... swallowed by alligators," Harkat grunted. "I won't let you risk your ... life any—"

"This is a pointless argument," Evanna interrupted. "I don't have the power to transport either of you back."

"But *you* were able to ... come here," Harkat argued. "You must be able to ... return."

"Things aren't as simple as they seem," Evanna said. "I can't explain it without revealing facts which I must keep secret. All I'll say is that I didn't get here the way you did, and I can't open a gateway between the reality you know and this one. Only Desmond Tiny can."

There was no point in quizzing her further – the witch, like Mr Tiny, couldn't be drawn on certain issues – so we dropped it. "Can you tell us anything about the quest we're on?" I asked instead. "Where we have to go next or what we must do?"

"I can tell you that I am to act as your guide on the next stretch of your adventure," Evanna said. "That's why I intervened — since I'm part of your quest, I can play an active role in it, at least for a while."

"You're coming with us?" I whooped, delighted at the thought of having someone to show us the way.

"Yes," Evanna smiled, "but only for a short time. I will be with you for ten, maybe eleven days. After that you're on your own." Rising, she started away from us. "You may rest now," she said. "Nothing will disturb your slumber here. I'll return in the afternoon and we'll set off."

"For where?" Harkat asked. But if the witch heard, she didn't bother to respond, and seconds later she was gone. Since there was nothing else we could do, Harkat and I made rough beds on the grass, lay down and slept.

# CHAPTER ELEVEN

AFTER BREAKFAST, Evanna guided us out of the swamp and south across more hard, barren land. It wasn't as lifeless as the desert we'd crossed, but very little grew on the reddish soil, and the animals were tough-skinned and bony.

Over the days and nights that followed, we slyly probed the witch for clues about where we were, who Harkat had been, what the gelatinous globes were for, and what lay ahead. We slid the questions into ordinary conversations, hoping to catch Evanna off guard. But she was sharp as a snake and never let anything slip.

Despite her annoying reluctance to reveal anything of our circumstances, she was a welcome travelling companion. She arranged the sleeping quarters every night – she could set up a camp within seconds – and told us what we could and couldn't eat (many of the animals and plants were poisonous or indigestible). She also spun tales and sung songs to amuse us during the long, harsh hours of walking.

I asked her several times how the War of the Scars was going, and what Vancha March and the other Princes and Generals were up to. She only shook her head at such questions and said this was not the time for her to comment.

We often discussed Mr Crepsley. Evanna had known the vampire long before I did and was able to tell me what he'd been like as a younger man. I felt sad talking about my lost friend, but it was a warm sort of sadness, not like the cold misery I experienced in the early weeks after he'd died. One night, when Harkat was asleep and snoring loudly (Evanna had confirmed what he'd already suspected – he could breathe the air here – so he'd dispensed with his mask), I asked Evanna if it was possible to communicate with Mr Crepsley. "Mr Tiny has the power to speak with the dead," I said. "Can you?"

"Yes," she said, "but we can only speak to those whose spirits remain trapped on Earth after they die. Most people's souls move on — though nobody knows for sure where they go, not even my father."

"So you can't get in touch with Mr Crepsley?" I asked.

"Thankfully, no," she smiled. "Larten has left the realm of the physical for ever. I like to think he is with Arra Sails and his other loved ones in Paradise, awaiting the rest of his friends."

Arra Sails was a female vampire. She and Mr Crepsley had been "married" once. She died when a vampire traitor –

Kurda Smahlt – sneaked a band of vampaneze into Vampire Mountain. Thinking about Arra and Kurda set me to pondering the past, and I asked Evanna if there'd been any way to avoid the bloody War of the Scars. "If Kurda had told us about the Lord of the Vampaneze, would it have made a difference? Or what if he'd become a Prince, taken control of the Stone of Blood and forced the Generals to submit to the vampaneze? Would Mr Crepsley be alive? And Arra? And all the others who've died in the war?"

Evanna sighed deeply. "Time is like a jigsaw puzzle," she said. "Imagine a giant box full of billions of pieces of millions of puzzles — that is the future. Beside it lies a huge board, partially filled with bits of the overall puzzle — that is the past. Those in the present reach blindly into the box of the future every time they have a decision to make, draw a piece of the puzzle out and slot it into place on the board. Once a piece has been added, it influences the final shape and design of the puzzle, and it's useless trying to fathom what the puzzle would have looked like if a different piece had been picked." She paused. "Unless you're Desmond Tiny. He spends most of his time considering the puzzle and contemplating alternative patterns."

I thought about that for a long time before speaking again. "What you're saying is that there's no point worrying about the past, because we can't change it?"

"Basically," she nodded, then leant over, one green eye shining brightly, one brown eye gleaming dully. "A mortal can drive himself mad thinking about the nature of the universal puzzle. Concern yourself only with the problems of the present and you will get along fine."

It was an odd conversation, one I returned to often, not just that night when I was trying to sleep, but during the quieter moments of the testing weeks ahead.

Eleven days after Evanna had rescued me from the jaws of the alligator, we came to the edge of an immense lake. At first I thought it was a sea – I couldn't see to the far side – but when I tested the water, I found it fresh, although very bitter.

"This is where I'll leave you," Evanna said, gazing out over the dark blue water, then up into the cloud-filled sky. The weather had changed during the course of our journey — clouds and rain were now the norm.

"What's the lake called?" Harkat asked, hoping – like me – that this was the Lake of Souls, though we both knew in our hearts that it wasn't.

"It has no name," Evanna said. "It's a relatively new formation, and the sentient beings of this planet have yet to discover it."

"You mean there are people here?" Harkat asked sharply.

"Yes," the witch replied.

"Why haven't we seen any?" I asked.

"This is a large planet," Evanna said, "but people are few. You may run into some before your adventure draws to a close, but don't get sidetracked — you're here to discover the truth about Harkat, not cavort with the natives. Now, would you like a hand making a raft, or would you rather do it yourselves?"

"What will we need a raft for?" I asked.

Evanna pointed to the lake. "Three guesses, genius."

"Can't we track around it?" Harkat enquired.

"You can, but I don't advise it."

We sighed — when Evanna said something like that, we knew we hadn't much of a choice. "What will we build it from?" I asked. "It's been a few days since I spotted any trees."

"We're close to the wreck of a boat," Evanna said, heading off to the left. "We can strip it bare and use the wood."

"I thought you said none of the … people here had found this lake," Harkat said, but if the witch heard the query, she paid it no heed.

About a kilometre up the pebbly lake shore, we found the bleached remains of a small wooden boat. The first planks we pulled off were soggy and rotten, but there were stronger planks underneath. We stacked them in a tidy pile, sorting them by length.

"How are we going to bind them?" I asked when we were ready to begin construction. "There aren't any nails." I wiped rain from my forehead — it had been drizzling steadily for the last hour.

"The builder of the boat used mud to bind the planks," Evanna said. "He had no rope or nails, and no intention of sailing the boat — he merely built it to keep himself busy."

"Mud won't keep a raft together once we … get out on the water," Harkat noted dubiously.

"Indeed," Evanna smirked. "That's why we are going to tie the planks tightly with ropes." The squat witch began unwrapping the ropes she kept knotted around her body.

"Do you want us to look away?" I asked.

"No need," she laughed. "I don't plan to strip myself bare!"

The witch reeled off an incredibly long line of rope, dozens of metres in length, yet the ropes around her body didn't diminish, and she was as discreetly covered when she stopped as she'd been at the outset. "There!" she grunted. "That should suffice."

We spent the rest of the day constructing the raft, Evanna acting as the designer, performing magical shortcuts when our backs were turned, making our job a lot quicker and easier than it should have been. It wasn't a large raft when finished, two and a half metres long by two wide, but we could both fit on it and lie down in comfort. Evanna wouldn't tell us how wide the lake was, but said we'd have to sail due south and sleep on the raft a few nights at least. The raft floated nicely when we tested it and although we had no sails, we fashioned oars out of leftover planks.

"You should be fine now," Evanna said. "You won't be able to light a fire, but fish swim close to the surface of the lake. Catch and eat them raw. And the water is unpleasant but safe to drink."

"Evanna…" I began, then coughed with embarrassment.

"What is it, Darren?" the witch asked.

"The gelatinous globes," I muttered. "Will you tell us what they're for?"

"No," she said. "And that's not what you wanted to ask. Out with it, please. What's bothering you?"

"Blood," I sighed. "It's been ages since I last drank human blood. I'm feeling the side effects — I've lost a lot of my sharpness and strength. If I carry on like this, I'll die. I was wondering if I could drink from *you*?"

Evanna smiled regretfully. "I would gladly let you drink from me, but I'm not human and my blood's not fit for consumption — you'd feel a lot worse afterwards! But don't worry. If the fates are kind, you'll find a feeding source shortly. If they're not," she added darkly, "you'll have greater problems to worry about.

"Now," the witch said, stepping away from the raft, "I must leave you. The sooner you set off, the sooner you'll arrive at the other side. I've just this to say — I've saved it until now because I had to — and then I'll depart. I can't tell you what the future has in store, but I can offer this advice — to fish in the Lake of Souls, you must borrow a net which has been used to trawl for the dead. And to access the Lake, you'll need the holy liquid from the Temple of the Grotesque."

"*Temple of the Grotesque?*" Harkat and I immediately asked together.

"Sorry," Evanna grunted. "I can tell you that much, but nothing else." Waving to us, the witch said, "Luck, Darren Shan. Luck, Harkat Mulds." And then, before we could reply, she darted away, moving with magical speed, disappearing out of sight within seconds into the gloom of the coming night.

Harkat and I stared at one another silently, then turned and manoeuvred our meagre stash of possessions on to the raft. We divided the gelatinous globes into three piles: one for Harkat, one for me and one in a scrap of cloth tied to the raft, then set off in the gathering darkness across the cold, still water of the nameless lake.

# CHAPTER TWELVE

WE ROWED for most of the night, in what we hoped was a straight line (there seemed to be no currents to drag us off course), rested for a few hours either side of dawn, then began rowing again, this time navigating south by the position of the sun. By the third day we were bored out of our skulls. There was nothing to do on the calm, open lake, and no change in scenery — dark blue underneath, mostly unbroken grey overhead. Fishing distracted us for short periods each day, but the fish were plentiful and easy to catch, and soon it was back to the rowing and resting.

To keep ourselves amused, we invented games using the teeth Harkat had pulled from the dead panther. There weren't many word games we could play with such a small complement of letters, but by giving each letter a number, we were able to pretend the teeth were dice and indulge in simple gambling games. We didn't have anything of value to bet, so we used the bones of the fish we caught as gambling chips, and made believe they were worth vast amounts of money.

During a rest period, as Harkat was cleaning the teeth – taking his time, to stretch the job out – he picked up a long incisor, the one marked by a K, and frowned. "This is hollow," he said, holding it up and peering through it. Putting it to his wide mouth, he blew through it, held it up again, then passed it to me.

I studied the tooth against the grey light of the sky, squinting to see better. "It's very smooth," I noted. "And it goes from being wide at the top to narrow at the tip."

"It's almost as though … a hole has been bored through it," Harkat said.

"How, and what for?" I asked.

"Don't know," Harkat said. "But it's the only one … like that."

"Maybe an insect did it," I suggested. "A parasite which burrows into an animal's teeth and gnaws its way upwards, feeding on the material inside."

Harkat stared at me for a moment, then opened his mouth as wide as he could and gurgled, "Check my teeth quick!"

"Mine first!" I yelped, anxiously probing my teeth with my tongue.

"Your teeth are tougher … than mine," he said. "I'm more vulnerable."

Since that was true, I leant forward to examine Harkat's sharp grey teeth. I studied them thoroughly, but there was no sign that any had been invaded. Harkat checked mine next, but

I drew a clean bill of health too. We relaxed after that — though we did a lot of prodding and jabbing with our tongues over the next few hours! — and Harkat returned to cleaning the teeth, keeping the tooth with the hole to one side, slightly away from the others.

That fourth night, as we slept after many hours of rowing, huddled together in the middle of the raft, we were woken by a thunderous flapping sound overhead. We bolted out of our sleep and sat up straight, covering our ears to drown out the noise. The sound was like nothing I'd heard before, impossibly heavy, as though a giant was beating clean his bed sheets. It was accompanied by strong, cool gusts of wind which set the water rippling and our raft rocking. It was a dark night with no break in the clouds, and we couldn't see what was making the noise.

"What is it?" I whispered. Harkat couldn't hear my whisper over the noise, so I repeated myself, but not too loudly, for fear of giving our position away to whatever was above.

"No idea," Harkat replied, "but there's something ... familiar about it. I've heard it before ... but I can't remember where."

The flapping sounds died away as whatever it was moved on, the water calmed and our raft steadied, leaving us shaken but unharmed. When we discussed it later, we reasoned it must have been some huge breed of bird. But in my gut, I sensed that wasn't the answer, and by Harkat's troubled expression and inability to fall back asleep, I was sure he sensed it too.

We rowed quicker than usual in the morning, saying little about the sounds we'd heard the night before, but gazing up often at the sky. Neither of us could explain why the noise had so alarmed us — we just felt that we'd be in big trouble if the creature came again, by the light of day.

We spent so much time staring up at the clouds that it wasn't until early afternoon, during a brief rest period, that we looked ahead and realized we were within sight of land. "How far do you think ... it is?" Harkat asked.

"I'm not sure," I answered. "Four or five kilometres?" The land was low-lying, but there were mountains further on, tall grey peaks which blended with the clouds, which was why we hadn't noticed them before.

"We can be there soon if we ... row hard," Harkat noted.

"So let's row," I grunted, and we set to our task with renewed vigour. Harkat was able to row faster than me – my strength was failing rapidly as a result of not having any human blood to drink – but I stuck my head down and pushed my muscles to their full capacity. We were both eager to make the safety of land, where at least we could find a bush to hide under if we were attacked.

We'd covered about half the distance when the air overhead reverberated with the same heavy flapping sounds that had interrupted our slumber. Gusts of wind cut up the water around us. Pausing, we looked up and spotted something hovering far above. It seemed small, but that was because it was a long way up.

"What the hell is it?" I gasped.

Harkat shook his head in answer. "It must be immense," he muttered, "for its wings to create ... this much disturbance from that high up."

"Do you think it's spotted us?" I asked.

"It wouldn't be hovering there otherwise," Harkat said.

The flapping sound and accompanying wind stopped and the figure swooped towards us with frightening speed, becoming larger by the second. I thought it meant to torpedo us, but it pulled out of its dive ten or so metres above the raft. Slowing its descent, it unfurled gigantic wings and flapped to keep itself steady. The sound was ear shattering.

"Is that ... what I ... think it is?" I roared, clinging to the raft as waves broke over us, eyes bulging out of my head, unable to believe that this monster was real. I wished with all my heart that Harkat would tell me I was hallucinating.

"Yes!" Harkat shouted, shattering my wishes. "I knew I ... recognized it!" The Little Person crawled to the edge of the raft to gaze at the magnificent but terrifying creature of myth. He was petrified, like me, but there was also an excited gleam in his green eyes. "I've seen it before ... in my nightmares," he croaked, his voice only barely audible over the flapping of the extended wings. "It's a *dragon!*"

# CHAPTER THIRTEEN

I'D NEVER in my life seen anything as wondrous as this dragon, and even though I was struck numb with fear, I found myself admiring it, unable to react to the threat it posed. Though it was impossible to accurately judge its measurements, its wingspan had to be twenty metres. The wings were a patchy light green colour, thick where they connected to its body, but thin at the tips.

The dragon's body was seven or eight metres from snout to the tip of its tail. It put me in mind of a snake's tapered body – it was scaled – though it had a round bulging chest which angled back towards the tail. Its scales were a dull red and gold colour underneath. From what I could see of the dragon's back, it was dark green on top, with red flecks. It had a pair of long forelegs, ending in sharp claws, and two shorter limbs about a quarter of the way from the end of its body.

Its head was more like an alligator's than a snake's, long

and flat, with two yellow eyes protruding from its crown, large nostrils, and a flexible lower jaw which looked like it could open wide to consume large animals. Its face was a dark purple colour and its ears were surprisingly small, pointed and set close to its eyes. It had no teeth that I could see, but the gums of its jaws looked hard and sharp. It had a long, forked tongue which flicked lazily between its lips as it hung in the air and gazed upon us.

The dragon observed us for a few more seconds, wings beating steadily, claws flexing, pupils opening and dilating. Then, tucking in its wings, it dived sharply, forelegs stretched, talons exposed, mouth closed — aiming for the raft!

With startled yells, Harkat and I snapped to attention and threw ourselves flat. The dragon screamed by overhead. One of its claws connected with my left shoulder and sent me crashing into Harkat.

As we pushed ourselves apart, I sat up, rubbing my bruised shoulder, and saw the dragon turn smoothly in the air, reverse and begin another dive. This time, instead of throwing himself on to the raft, Harkat grabbed his oar and thrust it up at the dragon, roaring a challenge at the monster. The dragon screeched angrily in reply – a high-pitched sound – and swerved away.

"Get up!" Harkat yelled at me. As I struggled to my feet, he thrust my oar into my hands, got to his knees and rowed desperately. "You keep it off … if you can," he gasped. "I'll try and get us … to shore. Our only hope is to … make land and hope we can … hide."

Holding the oar up was agony, but I ignored the pain in my shoulder and kept the piece of wood aloft, pointed at the dragon like a spear, silently willing Harkat to row even quicker. Above, the dragon circled, yellow eyes focused on the raft, occasionally screeching.

"It's assessing us," I muttered.

"What?" Harkat grunted.

"It's making a study. Noting our speed, analyzing our strengths, calculating our weaknesses." I lowered my oar. "Stop rowing."

"Are you crazy?" Harkat shouted.

"We'll never make it," I said calmly. "We're too far out. We'd best save our strength for fighting."

"How the hell do you think ... we're going to fight a dragon?" Harkat snorted.

"I don't know," I sighed. "But we can't out-pace it, so we might as well be fresh when it attacks."

Harkat stopped rowing and stood beside me, staring at the dragon with his unblinking green eyes. "Maybe it won't attack," he said with hollow optimism.

"It's a predator," I replied, "like the panther and alligators. It's not a question of *if* it will attack, but *when*."

Harkat looked from the dragon to the shore and licked his lips. "What if we swam? We wouldn't be as visible ... in the water. That might make it harder ... for it to grab us."

"True," I agreed, "but we wouldn't be able to defend ourselves. We won't jump unless we have to. In the meantime, let's sharpen our oars." Drawing one of my knives, I whittled away at the end of my oar. Harkat did the same with his. Within seconds of us setting to work on the oars, the dragon – perhaps sensing our intent – attacked, cutting short our preparations.

My immediate instinct was to duck, but I stood firm beside Harkat and we both raised our oars defensively. The dragon didn't pull out of its dive this time, but swooped even lower than before and barrelled into us with its hard head and shoulders, wings tucked in tight. We jabbed at it with our oars, but they snapped off its hard scales without causing the slightest bit of damage.

The dragon collided with the raft. The force of the blow sent us flying clear of the raft, deep under water. I came up gasping and thrashing wildly. Harkat was several metres adrift of me, also winded and bruised from the encounter. "Got to ... make the ... raft!" he shouted.

"No use!" I cried, pointing at the wreckage of the raft, which had been shattered to splinters. The dragon was hovering overhead, almost perpendicular to the sea, tail curled up into its scaly body. I swam to where Harkat was bobbing up and down, and we gazed up fearfully at the flying lizard.

"What's it waiting for?" Harkat wheezed. "We're at its mercy. Why isn't it finishing ... us off?"

"It seems to be puffing itself up," I noted, as the dragon closed its mouth and breathed in through its widening nostrils. "It's almost as though it's getting ready to..." I stopped, my face whitening. "Charna's guts!"

"What?" Harkat snapped.

"Have you forgotten what dragons are famous for?"

Harkat stared at me, clueless, then clicked to it. "They breathe fire!"

Our eyes locked on the dragon's chest, which was expanding steadily. "Watch it closely," I said, grabbing hold of Harkat's robes. "When I say 'dive', power for the bottom of the lake as hard as you can, and stay under till your breath runs out."

"It'll still be here ... when we come up," Harkat said dejectedly.

"Probably," I agreed, "but if we're lucky, it only has one burst of fire in it."

"What are you basing that ... judgement on?" Harkat asked.

"Nothing." I grinned shakily. "I'm just hoping."

There was no time for further exchanges. Above us, the dragon's tail curled down and back, and its head swung towards us. I waited until what I deemed the last possible instant, then, "*Dive!*" I screamed, and together Harkat and I rolled over and dived down deep, thrusting hard with our hands and feet.

As we descended, the water around us lit up redly. It then grew warm and began to bubble. Kicking even harder, we swam clear of the danger zone, down into the darkness of the deeper water. Once safe, we stopped and looked up. The lake had darkened again and we couldn't see the dragon. Clinging tight to each other, we held our mouths shut, waiting for as long as our breath would hold.

As we floated in silence and fear, there was a huge splash and the dragon came slicing through the water towards us. There was no time to evade it. Before we knew what was happening, the dragon hooked us with its claws, dragged us deeper down into the lake, then turned and struck for the surface.

Bursting free of the water, the dragon screeched triumphantly and rose into the air, Harkat trapped in one of its claws, me in the other. It had hold of my left arm, gripping me tightly, and I couldn't wriggle free.

"Darren!" Harkat screamed as we rose higher into the sky and surged towards shore. "Can you ... get loose?"

"No!" I shouted. "You?"

"I think so! It only has hold ... of my robes."

"Then free yourself!" I yelled.

"But what about—"

"Never mind me! Get free while you can!"

Harkat cursed bitterly, then grabbed hold of the back of his robes where the dragon had caught him, and tugged sharply. I didn't hear the ripping over the sound of the dragon's wings, but suddenly Harkat was free and falling, landing with an almighty splash in the lake beneath.

The dragon hissed with frustration and circled around, obviously meaning to go after Harkat again. We were almost over land now, at the very edge of the lake. "Stop!" I roared helplessly at the dragon. "Leave him alone!" To my astonishment, the dragon paused when I shouted, and gazed at me with a strange expression in its giant yellow eyes. "Leave him," I muttered desperately. Then, giving way to blind panic, I screamed at the beast, "Let me go, you son of a—"

Before I could complete the curse, the dragon's claws unexpectedly retracted, and suddenly I was dropping through the sky like a stone. I had just enough time to worry about whether I was over the lake or over land. Then I hit hard — *earth or water?* — and the world went black.

# CHAPTER FOURTEEN

WHEN MY eyes opened, I was lying in a hammock. I thought I was back in the Cirque Du Freak. I looked over to tell Harkat about a weird dream I'd had – full of black panthers, giant toads and dragons – but when I did, I saw that I was in a poorly built shack. There was a strange man standing close by, studying me with beady eyes and stroking a long curved knife.

"Who are you?" I shouted, falling out of the hammock. "Where am I?"

"Easy," the man chuckled, laying his knife aside. "Sorry t' trouble ye, young 'un. I was watching over ye while ye slept. We get an awful lot o' crabs and scorpions here. I didn't want 'em getting stuck into ye while ye was recovering. Harkat!" he bellowed. "Yer wee friend's awake!"

The door to the shack swung open and Harkat stepped in. The three scars from his fight with the panther were as prominent as usual, but he didn't look any the worse for wear otherwise. "Afternoon, Sleeping Beauty," he grinned. "You've been out for … almost two days."

"Where are we?" I asked, standing shakily. "And who's this?"

"Spits Abrams," the stranger introduced himself, stepping forward into the beam of sunlight shining through a large hole in the roof. He was a broad, bearded man of medium height, with small eyes and bushy eyebrows. His black hair was long and curly, tied back with coloured pieces of string. He wore a faded brown jacket and trousers, a dirty white vest, and knee-high black boots. He was smiling and I could see that he was missing several teeth, while the others were discoloured and jagged. "Spits Abrams," he said again, sticking out a hand. "Pleased t' meet ye."

I took the man's hand — he had a strong grip — and shook it warily, wondering who he was and how I'd wound up here.

"Spits rescued you from the lake," Harkat said. "He saw the dragon attack … and drop you. He dragged you out and was … waiting for you to dry when *I* waded out. He got a shock when … he saw me, but I convinced him I was harmless. We carried you here, to his … home. We've been waiting for you … to wake."

"Many thanks, Mr Abrams," I said.

"'Tain't nowt t' be thanking me fer," he laughed. "I jest fished ye out, same as any other fisherman would've."

"You're a fisherman?" I asked.

"Of a sort," he beamed. "I used t' be a pirate 'fore I ended up here, and 'twas people I fished fer. But since there ain't much grows round these parts, I've been eating mostly fish since I came — and fishing fer 'em."

"A pirate?" I blinked. "A real one?"

"Aaarrr, Darren lad," he growled, then winked.

"Let's go outside," Harkat said, seeing my confusion. "There's food on the fire and ... your clothes are dry and repaired."

I realized I was only wearing my underpants, so I hurried out after Harkat, found my clothes hanging on a tree, and slipped them on. We were close to the edge of the lake, on a meagre green patch amidst a long stretch of rocky soil. The shack was built in the shelter of two small trees. There was a tiny garden out back.

"That's where I grows me potatoes," Spits said. "Not fer eating — though I has one 'r two when I takes a fancy — but fer brewing poteen. My grandfather came from Connemara — in Ireland — and he used t' make a living from it. He taught me all his secrets. I never bothered before I washed up here — I prefer whisky — but since spuds is all I can grow, I has t' make do."

Dressed, I sat by the fire and Spits offered me one of the fish speared on sticks over the flames. Biting into the fish, I ate ravenously, silently studying Spits Abrams, not sure what to make of him.

"Want some poteen to wash that down with?" Spits asked.

"I wouldn't," Harkat advised me. "I tried it and it made ... my eyes water."

"I'll give it a miss then," I said. Harkat had a high tolerance for alcohol, and could drink just about anything. If the poteen had made his eyes water, it'd probably blow my head clean off my neck.

"Yerra, go on," Spits encouraged me, passing over a jug filled with a clear liquid. "It might blind ye, but 'twon't kill ye. 'Twill put hairs on yer chest!"

"I'm hairy enough," I chuckled, then leant forward, nudging the jug of poteen aside. "I don't want to be rude, Spits, but who are you and how did you get here?"

Spits laughed at the question. "That's what this 'un asked too, the first time he saw me," he said, pointing at Harkat with his thumb. "I've told him all about myself these last couple o' days — did a helluva lot o' talking fer a man who ain't said a word fer five or six years! I won't go through the whole thing again, just give ye the quick lowdown."

Spits had been a pirate in the Far East in the 1930s. Although piracy was a "dying art" (as he put it), there were still ships which sailed the seas and attacked others in the years before World War II, plundering them of their spoils. Spits found himself working on one of the pirate ships after years of ordinary naval service (he said he was shanghaied, though his eyes shifted cagily, and I got the feeling he wasn't being honest). "The *Prince o' Pariahs* was 'er name." He beamed proudly. "A fine ship, small but speedy. We was the scourge o' the waters wherever we went."

It was Spits's job to fish people out of the sea if they jumped in when they were boarded. "Two reasons we didn't like leaving 'em there," he said. "One was that we didn't want 'em to drown — we was pirates, not killers. The other was that the ones who jumped was normally carrying jewels or other such valuables — only the rich is that scared of being robbed!"

Spits got that shifty look in his eyes again when he was talking about fishing people out, but I said nothing about it, not wanting to offend the man who'd rescued me from the lake.

One night, the *Prince of Pariahs* found itself at the centre of a fierce storm. Spits said it was the worst he'd ever experienced, "and I been through just about everything that old sow of a sea can throw at a man!" As the ship broke apart, Spits grabbed a sturdy plank, some jugs of whisky and the nets he used to fish for people, and jumped overboard.

"Next thing I know, I'm in this lake," he finished. "I dragged myself out and there was a small man in big green galoshes waiting fer me." *Mr Tiny!* "He told me I'd come to a place far from the one I knew, and I was stuck. He said this was a land o' dragons, awful dangerous fer humans, but there was a shack where I'd be safe. If I stayed there and kept a watch on the lake, two people would come along eventually, and they could make my dreams come true. So I sat back, fished, found spuds growing nearby and brought some back fer me garden, and I been waiting ever since, five 'r six years near as I can figure."

I thought that over, staring from Spits to Harkat and back again. "What did he mean when he said we'd be able to make your dreams come true?" I asked.

"I suppose he meant ye'd be able t' get me home." Spits's eyes shifted nervously. "That's the only dream this old sailor has, t' get back where there's women and whisky, and not a drop o' water bigger than a puddle in sight — I've had enough o' seas and lakes!"

I wasn't sure I believed that was all the pirate had on his mind, but I let the matter drop and instead asked if he knew anything about the land ahead. "Not a whole lot," he answered. "I've done some exploring, but the dragons keep me pinned here most o' the time — I don't like wandering off too far with them demons waiting to pounce."

"There's more than one?" I frowned.

"Aaarrr," he said. "I ain't sure how many, but definitely four 'r five. The one that went after ye is the biggest I've seen, though mebbe there's bigger that don't bother with this lake."

"I don't like the sound of that," I muttered.

"Me neither," Harkat said. Then, turning to Spits, he said, "Show him the net."

Spits ducked behind the shack and emerged dragging a stringy old net, which he untangled and spread on the ground. "Two o' me nets slipped through with me," he said. "I lost t'other one a couple o' years back when a huge fish snatched it out o' my hands. I been keeping this 'un safe, in case of an emergency."

I remembered what Evanna had told us, that we'd need a net which had been used to fish for the dead if we were to find out who Harkat had been. "Think this is the net we need?" I asked Harkat.

"Must be," he answered. "Spits says he didn't use his nets to … fish for the dead, but this has to be it."

"Course I never fished fer the dead!" Spits boomed, laughing weakly. "What'd I do that fer? Mind, I been thinking about it since Harkat asked, and I recall a couple o' people who drowned when I was fishing 'em out. So I guess it probably *has* been used to drag up corpses — accidentally, like."

Spits's eyes practically shot out of his sockets, they were darting so swiftly from side to side. There was definitely something the ex-pirate wasn't telling us. But I couldn't pump him for information without indicating that I didn't believe him, and this was no time to risk making an enemy.

After eating, we discussed what to do next. Spits didn't know anything about a Temple of the Grotesque. Nor had he seen any people during his long, lonely years here. He'd told Harkat that the dragons usually approached the lake from the southeast. The Little Person was of the opinion that we should go in that direction, though he couldn't say why — just a gut feeling. Since I'd no personal preference, I bowed to his wishes and we agreed to head southeast that night, moving under cover of darkness.

"Ye'll take me along, won't ye?" Spits asked eagerly. "I'd feel awful if ye went without me."

"We don't know what we're ... walking into," Harkat warned the grizzly ex-pirate. "You could be risking your life ... by coming with us."

"Nowt t' worry about!" Spits guffawed. "'Twon't be the first time I risked it. I remember when the *Prince o' Pariahs* sailed into a trap off the Chinese coast..."

Once Spits got talking about his adventures on the pirate ship, there was no stopping him. He regaled us with wild, bawdy tales of the plundering they'd done and battles they'd engaged in. As he spoke, he sipped from his jug of poteen, and as the day wore on his voice got louder and his tales got wilder — he told some extra spicy stories about what he'd got up to during shore leave! Eventually, with the sun starting to set, he dozed off and curled up into a ball beside the fire, clutching his almost empty jug of poteen close to his chest.

"He's some character," I whispered, and Harkat chuckled softly.

"I feel sorry for him," Harkat said. "To be stuck here alone for ... so long must have been dreadful."

"Yes," I agreed, but not wholeheartedly. "But there's something 'off' about him, isn't there? He makes me feel uneasy, the way his eyes flick left and right so beadily when he's lying."

"I noticed that too," Harkat nodded. "He tells all sorts of lies – last night he ... said he'd been engaged to a Japanese princess – but it's ... only when he talks about his job on the ... *Prince of Pariahs* that he gets the *really* shifty look."

"What do you think he's hiding?" I asked.

"I've no idea," Harkat replied. "I doubt it matters — there are ... no pirate ships here."

"At least none that we've seen," I grinned.

Harkat studied the sleeping Spits — he was drooling into his unkempt beard — then said quietly, "We can leave him behind ... if you'd prefer. He'll be asleep for hours. If we leave now and walk ... fast, he'll never find us."

"Do you think he's dangerous?" I asked.

Harkat shrugged. "He might be. But there must be a reason why ... Mr Tiny put him here. I think we should take him. And his net."

"Definitely the net," I agreed. Clearing my throat, I added, "There's his blood too. I need human blood — and soon."

"I thought of that," Harkat said. "It's why I didn't stop him ... drinking. Do you want to take some now?"

"Maybe I should wait for him to wake and ask him," I suggested.

Harkat shook his head. "Spits is superstitious. He thinks I'm a demon."

"A demon!" I laughed.

"I told him what I really ... was, but he wouldn't listen. In the end I settled for persuading him ... that I was a harmless demon — an imp. I sounded him out about vampires. He believes in them, but thinks they're ... evil monsters. Said he'd drive a stake through ... the heart of the first one he met. I think you should drink ... from him while he's asleep, and never ... tell him what you really are."

I didn't like doing it — I'd no qualms about drinking secretly from strangers, but on the rare occasions when I'd had to drink from people I knew, I'd always asked their permission — but I bowed to Harkat's greater knowledge of Spits Abrams's ways.

Sneaking up on the sleeping sot, I bared his lower left leg, made a small cut with my right index nail, clamped my mouth around it and sucked. His blood was thin and riddled with alcohol — he must have drunk huge amounts of poteen and whisky over the years! — but I forced it down. When I'd drunk enough, I released him and waited for the blood around the cut to dry. When it had, I cleaned it and rolled the leg of his trousers down.

"Better?" Harkat asked.

"Yes." I burped. "I wouldn't like to drink from him often — there's more poteen than blood in his veins! — but it'll restore my strength and keep me going for the next few weeks."

"Spits won't wake until morning," Harkat noted. "We'll have to wait … until tomorrow night to start, unless you … want to risk travelling by day."

"With dragons roaming overhead? No thanks! Anyway, an extra day of rest won't hurt — I'm still recovering from our last run-in."

"By the way, how did you … get it to drop you?" Harkat asked as we settled down for the night. "And why did it … fly away and leave us?"

I thought back, recalled yelling at the dragon to let me go, and told Harkat what had happened. He stared at me disbelievingly, so I winked and said, "I always did have a way with dumb animals!" And I left it at that, even though I was equally bewildered by the dragon's strange retreat.

# CHAPTER FIFTEEN

I THOUGHT Spits would have a sore head when he awoke, but he was in fine form — he said he never suffered from hangovers. He spent the day tidying up the shack, putting everything in order in case he ever returned. He stashed a jug of poteen away in a corner and packed the rest in a large sack he planned to carry slung over his shoulder, along with spare clothes, his fishing net, some potatoes and dried fish slices. Harkat and I had almost nothing to carry – apart from the panther's teeth and gelatinous globes, most of which we'd managed to hang on to – so we offered to divide Spits's load between us, but he wouldn't hear of it. "Every man to a cross of his own," he muttered.

We took it easy during the day. I hacked my hair back from my eyes with one of Spits's rusty blades. We'd replaced our handmade knives, most of which we'd lost in the lake, with real knives that Spits had lying around.

Harkat stitched together holes in his robes with bits of old string.

When night fell, we set off, heading due southeast towards a mountain range in the distance. Spits was surprisingly morose to be leaving his shack – "'Tis the closest thing to a home I've had since running away t' sea when I was twelve," he sighed – but several swigs of poteen improved his mood and by midnight he was singing and joking.

I was worried that Spits would collapse – his legs were wobbling worse than the jelly-like globes we were carting – but as drunk as he got, his pace never wavered, though he did stop quite often to "bail out the bilge water". When we made camp beneath a bushy tree in the morning, he fell straight asleep and snored loudly all day long. He woke shortly before sunset, licked his lips and reached for the poteen.

The weather worsened over the next few nights, as we left the lowlands and scaled the mountains. It rained almost constantly, harder than before, soaking our clothes and leaving us wet, cold and miserable — except Spits, whose poteen warmed and cheered him up whatever the conditions. I decided to try some of Spits's home-brewed concoction, to see if it would combat the gloom. One swallow later, I was rolling on the ground, gasping for breath, eyes bulging. Spits laughed while Harkat poured water down my throat, then urged me to try it again. "The first dram's the worst," he chuckled. Through wheezing coughs, I firmly declined.

It was difficult to know what to make of Spits Abrams. A lot of the time he came across as a funny old sailor, crude and coarse, but with a soft centre. But as I spent more time with him, I thought that a lot of his speech patterns seemed deliberately theatrical — he spoke with a broad accent on purpose, to give the impression he was scatterbrained. And there were times when his mood darkened and he'd mutter ominously about people who'd betrayed him in one way or another.

"They thought they was so high and mighty!" he growled one night, weaving drunkenly under the cloudy sky. "Better than dumb old Spits. Said I was a monster, not fit t' share a ship with 'em. But I'll show 'em! When I gets me hands on 'em, I'll make 'em suffer!"

He never said how he intended to "get his hands on" whoever "'em" were. We hadn't told Spits what year we'd come from, but he knew time had moved on — he often made reference to "yer generation" or said "things was different in my day". I couldn't see any way back for Spits, and he couldn't either — a common refrain of his when he was feeling sorry for himself was, "Here I is and here I'll die." Yet still he swore to get his own back on "them what done me wrong", despite the fact that the people he disliked would have been dead and buried decades ago.

Another night, while he was telling us about his tasks on board the *Prince of Pariahs*, he stopped and looked at us with a steady blank expression. "I had t' kill every now and then," he said softly. "Pirates is vagabonds. Even though we didn't kill those we robbed, we sometimes had t'. If people refused t' surrender, we had t' put a stop to 'em. Couldn't afford t' let 'em off the hook."

"But I thought you didn't board the ships you attacked," I said. "You told us you fished out people who jumped overboard."

"Aaarrr," he grinned bleakly, "but a man in the water can struggle just as much as one on deck. A woman too. Sometimes I had t' teach 'em a lesson." His eyes cleared a little and he grinned sheepishly. "But that was rare. I only mention it so ye know ye can rely on me if we gets into a tight spot. I ain't a killer, but I'll do it if me back's against a wall, or t' save a friend."

Harkat and I didn't doze much that day. Instead we kept a wary watch on the snoring Spits. Although we were stronger and fitter than him, he posed a worrying threat. What if he got into a drunken fit and took it into his head to kill us in our sleep?

We discussed the possibility of leaving the ex-pirate behind, but it didn't seem fair to strand him in the mountains. Although he was able to keep pace beside us during our marches, he had no sense of direction and would have become lost in no time if he'd been by himself. Besides, we might have need of his fishing skills if we made it to the Lake of Souls. Both of us could catch fish with our hands, but neither of us knew much about angling.

In the end we chose to keep Spits with us, but agreed not to turn our backs on him, to take turns sleeping, and to cut him loose if he ever threatened violence.

We made slow but steady progress through the mountains. If the weather had been finer, we'd have raced through, but all the rain had led to mudslides and slippery underfoot conditions. We had to walk carefully, and were often forced to backtrack and skirt around an area made inaccessible by the rain and mud.

"Does it normally rain this much?" I asked Spits.

"T' tell the truth, this has been one o' the better years," he chortled. "We gets very hot summers — long, too — but the winters are dogs. Mind, it'll probably break in another night or two — we ain't hit the worst o' the season yet, and it's rare t' get more'n a week or so o' nonstop rain at this time o' year."

As though the clouds had been listening, they eased up the next morning — affording us a welcome view of blue sky — and by night, when we set off, it was the driest it had been since we landed at Spits's shack.

That same night, we topped a small peak and found ourselves on a sharp decline into a long, wide chasm leading out of the mountain ridges. The base of the chasm was flooded with rainwater, but there were ledges along the sides which we'd be able to use. Hurrying down the mountain, we located one of the broader ledges, tied a rope around ourselves to form a chain, me in front, Spits in the middle, Harkat behind, and set off over the fast-flowing river, edging forwards at a snail's pace. Spits even went so far as to cork his jug of poteen and leave it untouched!

Day dawned while we were on the ledge. We hadn't seen any caves in the cliff, but there were plenty of large holes and cracks. Untying ourselves, each of us crawled into a hole to rest, out of sight of any passing dragons. It was extremely uncomfortable, but I was exhausted after the hard climb and fell asleep immediately, not waking until late in the day.

After a quick meal – the last of Spits's dried fish slices – we tied ourselves together again and set off. It began to drizzle shortly afterwards, but then it cleared for the rest of the night and we progressed without interruption. The ledge didn't run all the way to the end of the chasm, but there were ledges above and beneath it which we were able to transfer to, making the journey in stages. Shortly before daybreak we came to the end of the chasm and crawled down to a flat plain which spread out for many kilometres ahead of us, ending in a massive forest which stretched left and right as far as we could see.

We debated our options. Since none of us wanted to sleep in a hole in the cliff again, and the route to the forest was littered with bushes we could hide under if we spotted a dragon, we decided to head for the trees straightaway. Forcing our tired legs on, we jogged briskly over the plain, Spits feeding himself with poteen, somehow managing not to spill a drop despite the jolting of his arms as he ran.

We made camp just within the edge of the forest. While Harkat kept an eye on Spits, I slept soundly until early afternoon. Harkat and I caught a wild pig soon after that, which Spits gleefully roasted over a quickly constructed fire. We tucked into our first hot meal since leaving for the mountains more than two weeks earlier — delicious! Wiping our hands clean on the grass afterwards, we set off in a general southeast direction – it was hard to tell precisely with all the tree cover – prepared for a long, gloomy trek through the forest.

To our surprise, we cleared the trees a few hours before sunset — the forest was long, but narrow. We found ourselves standing at the top of a small cliff, gazing down on fields of the tallest, greenest grass I'd ever seen. No trees grew in the fields, and though there must have been many streams feeding the soil to produce such greenery, they were hidden by the towering stalks of grass.

Only one object stood out against the otherwise unbroken sea of green — a huge white building a couple of kilometres directly ahead, which shone like a beacon under the evening sun. Harkat and I shared a glance and said simultaneously, with a mixture of excitement and tension, "The Temple of the Grotesque!"

Spits stared suspiciously at the building, spat over the edge of the cliff, and snorted. "Trouble!"

# CHAPTER SIXTEEN

THE STALKS of grass grew thickly together, a couple of metres high. We had to chop our way through, like hacking a path through a jungle. It was hard, slow work, and night had fallen before we reached the temple. Studying it by the light of a strong moon, we were impressed by its stature. Made of large rough stones which had been painted white, it stood thirty-five or forty metres high. A square building, its walls were about a hundred metres in length, and supported a flat roof. We did a full circuit of the exterior and there was only one entrance, a huge open doorway, five metres wide by eight or nine high. We could see the flicker of candlelight from within.

"I don't like the look o' this place," Spits muttered.

"Me neither," I sighed. "But if it's the Temple of the Grotesque, we have to go in and find the holy liquid that Evanna told us about."

"Ye two can trust a witch's word if ye like," Spits grunted, "but I ain't having nowt t' do with dark forces! If ye want t' enter, best o' luck. I'll wait out here."

"Afraid?" Harkat grinned.

"Aaarrr," Spits replied. "Ye should be too. Ye can call this the Temple o' the Grotesque if ye like, but I knows what it really is — a Temple o' Death!" And he stormed off to find a hiding place in a patch of nearby grass.

Harkat and I shared Spits's gloomy opinion, but we had to venture in. Knives drawn, we crept to the doorway and were about to enter, when the sound of chanting drifted to us over the clear night air. We paused uncertainly, then drew back to where Spits was hiding in the grass.

"Changed yer minds?" he hooted.

"We heard something," Harkat told him. "It sounded like voices — *human* . . . voices. They were chanting."

"Where'd they come from?" Spits asked.

"To our left," I told him.

"Will I go check 'em out while ye explore yer temple?"

"I think it would be best if we all . . . went to check," Harkat said. "If there are people here, this temple . . . must be theirs. We can ask them about it and . . . maybe they can help us."

"Ye're awfully simple-minded fer a demon," Spits laughed cynically. "Never trust a stranger, that's what I says!"

That was good advice, and we paid heed to it, quietly sliding through the grass — which didn't grow so thickly here — cautiously closing in on the chanting. A short way beyond the temple, we came to the edge of a clearing. In it was a small, peculiar-looking village. The huts were made of grass and built very low to the ground, no more than a metre high. Either we'd come to a village of pygmies, or the huts were only used as shelters to sleep beneath. Rough grey robes were bundled in a pile in the centre of the village. Dead sheep-like animals were stacked one on top of another, close to the robes.

As we were taking in the sight of the village, a naked man appeared through the grass to our right. He was of ordinary height and build, a light brown colour, but with lanky pink hair and dull white eyes. He walked to the mound of dead sheep, dragged one out and returned the way he'd come, pulling the sheep by its rear legs. Without discussing it, Spits, Harkat and I set off after him, keeping to the edge of the village, still hidden in the grass.

The chanting — which had died down — began again as we approached the spot where the man had disappeared into the grass. We found a path of many footprints in the soft earth and traced them to a second, smaller clearing. There was a pond at the centre, around which thirty-seven people stood, eight men, fifteen women and fourteen children. All were naked, brown-skinned, pink-haired and white-eyed.

Two men hung the dead sheep over the pond, stretched lengthways by its legs, while another man took a knife of white bone or stone and sliced the animal's stomach open. Blood and guts plopped into the pond. As I strained my neck, I saw that the water was a dirty red colour. The men held the sheep over the pond until the blood stopped dripping, then slung the carcass to one side and stood back as three women stepped forward.

The women were old and wrinkled, with fierce expressions and bony fingers. Chanting louder than anyone else, they stooped, swirled the water of the pond around with their hands, then filled three leather flasks with it. Standing, they beckoned the other people forward. As they filed past the first woman, she raised her flask high and poured the red water over their heads. The second woman wet her fingers with the water and drew two rough circular diagrams on everybody's chest. The third pressed the mouth of her flask to their lips, and they drank the putrid water within.

After the three women had attended to all of the people, they moved in a line back to the village, eyes closed, chanting softly. We slipped off to one side, then trailed after them, frightened and perplexed, but incredibly curious.

In the village, the people pulled on the grey robes, each of which was cut away in front to reveal their chest and the round crimson signs. Only one person remained unclothed — a young boy, of about twelve or thirteen. When all were dressed, they formed a long line, three abreast, the trio of old women who'd handled the flasks at the fore and the naked boy by himself in front of everybody else. Chanting loudly, they marched in a procession towards the temple. We waited until they'd passed, then followed silently, intrigued.

At the entrance to the temple, the procession stopped and the volume of the chanting increased. I couldn't understand what they were saying – their language was alien to me – but one word was repeated more than any other, and with great emphasis. "Kulashka!"

"Any idea what 'Kulashka' means?" I asked Harkat and Spits.

"No," Harkat said.

Spits began to shake his head, then stopped, eyes widening, lips thinning with fear. "Saints o' the sailors!" he croaked, and fell to his knees.

Harkat and I gawped at Spits, then looked up and saw the cause of his shock. Our jaws dropped as we set eyes on the most nightmarishly monstrous creature imaginable, wriggling out of the temple like a mutant worm.

It must have been human once, or descended from humans. It had a human face, except its head was the size of six or seven normal heads. And it had dozens of hands. No arms — and no legs or feet — just loads of hands sticking out of it like pin heads in a pincushion. It was a couple of metres wide and maybe ten or eleven metres long. Its body tapered back like a giant slug. It crept forward slowly on its hundreds of fingers, dragging itself along, though it looked capable of moving more quickly if it wished. It had just one enormous bloodshot eye, hanging low on the left side of its face. Several ears dotted its head in various places, and there were two huge, bulging noses set high above its upper lip. Its skin was a dirty white colour, hanging from its obscene frame in saggy, flabby folds, which quivered wildly every time it moved.

Evanna had named the monster well. It was utterly and

totally grotesque. No other word could have conveyed its repulsive qualities as simply and clearly.

As I recovered from my initial shock, I focused on what was happening. The naked boy was on his knees beneath the Grotesque, arms spread wide, roaring over and over, "Kulashka! Kulashka! Kulashka!"

As the boy roared and the people chanted, the Grotesque paused and raised its head. It did this like a snake, arching its body back so that the front section came up. From where we were hiding I got a closer look at its face. It was lumpy and ill formed, as though it had been carved from putty by a sculptor with a shaky hand. There were scraps of hair everywhere I looked, nasty dark tufts, more like skin growths than hair. I saw no teeth inside its gaping maw of a mouth, except for two long, curved fangs near the front.

The Grotesque lowered itself and slithered around the group of people. It left a thin, slimy trail of sweat. The sweat oozed from pores all over its body. I caught the salty scent, and although it wasn't as overpowering as that of the giant toad, it was enough to make me clamp my hand over my nose and mouth so that I didn't throw up. The people — the Kulashkas, for want of a better word — didn't mind the stench though. They knelt as their ... god? king? pet? ... whatever it was to them, passed and rubbed their faces in its trail of sweat. Some even stuck out their tongues and licked it up!

When the Grotesque had circled all of its worshippers, it returned to the boy at the front. Raising its head again, it leant forward and stuck out its tongue, a huge pink slab, dripping with thick globs of saliva. It licked the boy's face. He didn't flinch, but smiled proudly. The Grotesque licked him again, then wrapped its unnatural body around him once, twice, three times, and suffocated him with its fleshy coils, the way a boa constrictor kills its victims.

My first impulse was to rush to the boy's aid when I saw him disappearing beneath the sweaty flesh of the Grotesque, but I couldn't have saved him. Besides, I could see that he didn't wish to be saved. It was clear by his smile that he considered this an honour. So I stayed crouched low in the grass and kept out of it.

The Grotesque crushed the life out of the boy – he cried out once, briefly, as the creature made splinters of his bones – then unwrapped itself and set about swallowing him whole. Again, in this respect, it acted like a snake. It had a supple lower jaw which stretched down far enough for the monster to get its mouth around the boy's head and shoulders. By using its tongue, jaw and some of its hands, it slowly but steadily fed the rest of the boy's body down its eager throat.

As the Grotesque devoured the boy, two of the women entered the temple. They emerged shortly afterwards, clasping two glass vials, about forty centimetres long, with thick glass walls and cork stoppers. A dark liquid ran about three-quarters of the way to the top of each vial — it had to be Evanna's "holy liquid".

When the Grotesque had finished devouring the boy, a man stepped forward and took one of the vials. Stepping up to the beast, he held the vial aloft and chanted softly. The Grotesque studied him coldly. I thought it meant to kill him too, but then it lowered its head and opened its enormous mouth. The man reached into the Grotesque's mouth, removed the cork from the vial and raised it to one of the creature's fangs. Inserting the tip of the fang into the vial, he pressed the glass wall hard against it. A thick, viscous substance oozed out of the fang and trickled down the side of the tube. I'd seen Evra milking poison from his snake's fangs many times — this was exactly the same.

When no more liquid seeped from the fang, the man corked the vial, handed it back to the woman, took the second vial and milked the Grotesque's other fang. When he'd finished, he stepped away and the monster's mouth closed. The man passed the vial back, joined the rest of the group, and began chanting loudly along with everyone else. The Grotesque studied them with its single red eye, its inhumanly human-like head swaying from side to side in time with the chanting. Then it slowly turned and scuttled back into the temple on its carriage of fingers. As it entered, the people followed, in rows of three, chanting softly, vanishing into the gloom of the temple after the Grotesque, leaving us shaken and alone outside, to withdraw and discuss the sinister spectacle.

# CHAPTER SEVENTEEN

"YE'RE CRAZY!" Spits hissed, keeping his voice down so as not to attract the attention of the Kulashkas. "Ye want t' go into that devil's lair and risk yer lives, fer the sake o' some bottles o' poison?"

"There must be something ... special about it," Harkat insisted. "We wouldn't have been told we ... needed it if it wasn't important."

"Nowt's worth throwing yer lives away fer," Spits snarled. "That monster will have ye both fer pudding, and still be hungry after."

"I'm not sure about that," I muttered. "It fed like a snake. I know about snakes from when I shared a tent with Evra — a snake-boy," I added for Spits's benefit. "A child would take a long time to digest, even for a beast of that size. I doubt it'll need to eat again for a few days. And a snake normally sleeps while it's digesting."

"But this ain't a snake," Spits reminded me. "It's a ... what did ye call it?"

"Grotesque," Harkat said.

"Aaarrr. Ye never shared a tent with a Grotesque, did ye? So ye know nothing about 'em. Ye'd be mad t' risk it. And what about that crazy pink-haired mob? If they catch ye, they won't be long offering ye up t' that giant mongrel o' theirs."

"What do you think the deal ... is with them?" Harkat asked. "I believe they worship the Grotesque. That's why they ... sacrificed the boy."

"A fine how-d'ye-do!" Spits huffed. "'Tis one thing t' go killing a stranger, but t' willingly give up one o' yer own — madness!"

"They can't do it often," I noted. "There aren't many of them. They'd die out if they made a human sacrifice every time the beast was hungry. They must feed it with sheep and other animals, and only offer up a human on special occasions."

"Should we try ... talking to them?" Harkat asked. "Many civilized people in the past ... offered human sacrifices to their gods. They might not be violent."

"I've no intention of putting them to the test," I said quickly. "We can't walk away from this — we saw them milk the snake's fangs, and I'm pretty certain that poison is the holy liquid we need. But let's not push our luck. There's no telling what the people of this world are like. The Kulashkas might be lovely folk who welcome strangers with open arms — or they might feed us to the Grotesque the instant they set eyes on us."

"We're stronger than them," Harkat said. "We could fight them off."

"We don't know that," I disagreed. "We've no idea what these people are capable of. They could be ten times as strong as you or me. I say we hit the temple, grab the vials, and beat it quick."

"Forget the vials!" Spits pleaded. He'd been drinking heavily from his jug since we'd retreated to safety and was trembling worse than normal. "We can come back later if we need 'em."

"No," Harkat said. "Darren's right about the Kulashkas. But if we're going to launch a ... quick raid, we need to do it while the Grotesque is sleeping. We have to go after the ... holy liquid now. You don't have to come ... if you don't want."

"I won't!" Spits said quickly. "I ain't gonna chuck my life away on a crazy thing like this. I'll wait out here. If ye don't return, I'll carry on ahead and look fer yer Lake o' Souls myself. If it holds the dead like ye say, I might meet ye there!" He chuckled wickedly at that.

"Will we go while it's dark," I asked Harkat, "or wait for morning?"

"Wait," Harkat said. "The Kulashkas might have sung themselves ... to sleep by then." The pink-haired people had returned to their village an hour after making their sacrifice, and had been singing, dancing and chanting ever since.

We lay back and rested as the moon crossed the cloudless sky (typical — when we wanted clouds for cover, there weren't any!), listening to the music of the strange Kulashkas. Spits kept sipping from his jug of poteen, his beady eyes getting smaller and smaller, tugging at the strands of his tied-back hair, muttering darkly about block-headed fools and their just comeuppances.

The noise from the Kulashka village died away towards morning, and by dawn there was silence. Harkat and I shared a questioning glance, nodded and stood. "We're going," I told Spits, who was half dozing over his jug.

"Wha'?" he grunted, head snapping up.

"We're going," I said again. "Wait here. If we're not back by night, go your own way and don't worry about us."

"I won't wait that long," he sniffed. "I'll be gone by midday, with 'r without ye."

"Suit yourself," I sighed, "but you'd be less visible in the dark. It would be safer."

Spits's features softened. "Ye're mad," he said, "but ye've more guts than any pirate I ever sailed with. I'll wait till sunset and keep the poteen ready — ye might be glad of it if ye survive."

"We might at that," I grinned, then spun away with Harkat and pushed through the tall covering grass to the doorway of the Temple of the Grotesque.

We stopped at the door of the temple, gripping our knives close by our sides, inhaling the foul sweaty stench of the beast. "What if there are guards?" I whispered.

"Knock them out," Harkat said. "Kill them only if we ... must. But I doubt there'll be any — they would have ... come out with the Grotesque if there were."

Taking deep, nervous breaths, we slid inside the temple, back to back, moving slowly and warily. Candles jutted from the walls, not a huge number, but enough to light our way. We were in a short, narrow corridor, covered by a low roof. A large room lay ahead. We paused at the entrance. The room was enormous. The roof was supported by giant pillars, but there were no other dividing structures. In the centre of the temple, the Grotesque was curled around a raised circular platform, upon which we saw a tall, hollow, upright crystal cylinder packed with vials like the ones the Kulashkas had used to milk the monster's venom.

"No lack of holy liquid," I whispered to Harkat.

"The trouble will be … getting to it," he replied. "I think the Grotesque's body goes … all the way around the altar."

I hadn't thought of the platform as an altar, but now that I looked again, I saw that Harkat was right — the cylinder holding the vials had the appearance of some religious relic.

We started across the room to the altar, the only sound our shallow breathing. The Grotesque's head was buried underneath its fleshy rear, so it shouldn't have a view of us if it was awake — though I hoped with all my being that it wasn't! There was a path leading directly from the doorway to the altar, lit by tall candles, but we approached the altar from the side, where we'd be less conspicuous.

We soon ran into an unexpected obstacle. The floorboards at the sides of the path were rotten and creaked heavily as we crossed them. "The path must be the only one reinforced from below," I hissed as we stopped to ponder our options. "By the echoes of the creaks, there's a pit beneath the boards."

"Should we return to … the path?" Harkat asked.

I shook my head. "Let's continue — but tread carefully!"

Despite our attempts to proceed with care, a few metres further on, Harkat's left foot snapped through a board and his leg shot down into darkness. He gasped painfully but bit down on a cry. My eyes snapped to where the Grotesque was coiled, to see if it had stirred, but it was in the same position as before. The fingers close to its head twitched a few times — I hoped that meant it was asleep and dreaming.

Stooping, I examined the board around Harkat's leg, carefully snapped more of it away to increase the width of the hole, then helped ease him out of it and back on to slightly sturdier boards.

"Are you hurt?" I asked softly.

"Cut," Harkat answered, probing his leg. "Not bad."

"We can't chance these boards any longer," I said. "We'll have to use the path."

Together we hobbled back to the path, where we rested a minute, before advancing to the altar. By the luck of the vampires the Grotesque slept on. Once there, we walked around the putrid monster, looking for a gap where we could mount the altar. But the Grotesque had fully encircled it, chunks of its flesh draped off it in places. This close to the beast, I couldn't help but stare and marvel that such a thing could have come to exist. What troubled me most was its obviously human features. It was like a nightmare come to life — but a human nightmare. What was its history? How had it been born?

Having walked around the Grotesque a couple of times, I tore my gaze away. Not daring to talk this close to the creature,

I tucked my knife away and made hand signals at Harkat, indicating that we'd have to jump over the monster at its narrowest point, close to where its tail lapped over its head. Harkat didn't look thrilled with that idea, but there was no other way of getting to the altar, so he nodded reluctantly. I made a second set of hand signals, to the effect that I could jump and Harkat should remain where he was, but he shook his head and held up two stubby grey fingers, to show we should both go.

I jumped first. I crouched low, then leapt over the muscular coils of the giant beast. I landed softly, but spun quickly, not wishing to stand with my back to the Grotesque. It hadn't moved. Stepping aside, I nodded for Harkat to join me. He didn't leap quite as smoothly, but his feet cleared the monster, and I caught him as he landed, steadying him and muffling the sound.

We checked to make sure we hadn't disturbed the Grotesque, then faced the tall cylinder and studied the vials resting on see-through shelves within. Those at the top hadn't been filled, but there were dozens underneath, heavy with the thick poison from the Grotesque's fangs. The Kulashkas must have been milking the giant for decades to have amassed such a collection.

There was a frosty crystal front to the cylinder. I eased it open, reached inside, and pulled out a vial. It was cool and surprisingly heavy. I slipped it inside my shirt, pulled out a second vial and passed it to Harkat. He held it up to the light of the candles, scrutinizing the liquid inside.

As I was reaching for more vials, there was a shout from just inside the temple door. Looking up, startled, we saw two

Kulashka children, a boy and girl. I raised my fingers to my lips and waved at the children, hoping they'd stop shouting, but that only agitated them more. The girl turned and shot out the doorway, doubtless fleeing to wake the adults. The boy remained and raced towards us, yelling and clapping, grabbing a candle to use as a weapon.

I knew instantly that we'd have to forget the rest of the vials. Our only hope was to get out quick, before the Grotesque awoke or the Kulashkas poured into the temple. The pair of vials we'd stolen would have to do. Leaving the door of the cylinder hanging open, I stepped down to where Harkat was waiting and we got ready to jump. But before we could leap, the Grotesque's rear section swished back, its head whipped up, and we found ourselves gazing straight into its furious red eye — and at its bared, sabre-like fangs!

# CHAPTER EIGHTEEN

WE FROZE on the altar, mesmerized by the Grotesque's glinting, demonic eye. As we stood rooted, helpless, its body unfurled and its head rose a metre or two, arcing backwards. It was preparing to attack, but by raising its head, it broke eye contact with us. We snapped out of our daze, realized what was about to happen, and dropped to the floor as the monster struck.

One of the Grotesque's long fangs caught me between my shoulder blades as I hit the floor. It dug into my flesh and ripped down my back. I yelled with pain and fear, rolled over as the beast released me, and slithered behind the crystal cylinder.

The Grotesque jabbed at me as I retreated but missed. It let out a bellow, like a giant baby's angry cry, then turned on Harkat. He was lying on his back, with his face and stomach exposed, an easy target. The Grotesque raised itself up to strike. Harkat got ready to throw his vial of poison at it. The Grotesque shrieked fiercely and withdrew a couple of metres, the fingers near its tail carrying it away from Harkat, the fingers near its head wriggling at him like dozens of snakes or eels. A detached part of me noticed that there were small holes on each finger where its nails would be if it was human, and the sweat came out of these holes in steady streams.

Harkat scrambled around to where I was sheltering. "My back!" I gasped, turning so that he could examine it. "How bad is it?"

Harkat studied my wound swiftly, then grunted. "It's not very deep. It'll leave the mother of … all scars, but it won't kill you."

"Unless there was poison in the fang," I muttered.

"The Kulashkas milked it," Harkat said. "Fresh poison couldn't … have formed already — could it?"

"Not in a snake," I said, "but there's no telling with this thing."

I had no time to worry about it. The Grotesque slid around the altar, to attack us again. We backpedalled, keeping the cylinder between us and the Grotesque's bobbing head.

"Any plans for … getting out?" Harkat asked, drawing a knife but keeping his vial of poison in his left hand.

"I'm taking this second by second," I panted.

We retreated steadily, circling around the cylinder again and again, the monster following impatiently, spitting and growling, its tongue flicking between its lips, ready to strike the instant we relaxed our guard. The Kulashka boy was standing on the path to the altar, cheering the Grotesque on.

A minute later, the rest of the Kulashkas poured into the temple. Most were carrying weapons, and their faces were filled with fury. Hurrying to the altar, they spread out around it, crawled over the Grotesque and moved in on us, murder in their angry white eyes.

"This would be a good time to try talking to them," I said sarcastically to Harkat, but he took my wry advice seriously.

"We mean no harm!" he shouted. "We want to be ... your friends."

The Kulashkas stopped and murmured with astonishment when Harkat spoke. One of the men — I guessed it was their chief — stepped ahead of the others and pointed a spear at us. He shouted a question at Harkat but we couldn't understand what he was saying.

"We don't speak your language," I said, following Harkat's lead, keeping one eye on the man and one on the Grotesque, which was still scrabbling after us, though it had pulled back slightly to make room for the Kulashkas. The chief shouted at us again, but slower this time, emphasizing each word. I shook my head. "We can't understand you!" I cried.

"Friends!" Harkat tried desperately. "Amigos! Comrades! Buddies!"

The Kulashka stared at us uncertainly. Then his expression hardened and he barked something at the rest of his clan. Nodding, they advanced, their weapons raised offensively, herding us towards the fangs of the giant Grotesque.

I stabbed at one of the Kulashka women with my knife, a warning gesture, trying to ward her off, but she ignored me

149

and continued to close in, along with the others. Even the children were converging on us, small knives and spears held fast in their tiny hands.

"Let's try the poison!" I screamed at Harkat, pulling out my vial. "They might scatter if we throw it at their eyes!"

"OK!" he roared, and held his vial up high.

When the Kulashkas saw the vial in Harkat's grey hand, they froze with fear and most took a hasty step backwards. I was confused by their reaction, but seized on their fear and raised mine as well. When they saw another of the vials, the men, women and children spilt back off the platform, chattering fearfully, wildly waving their hands and weapons at us.

"What's going on?" I asked Harkat.

"They're afraid of the ... poison," he said, waving his vial at a handful of the Kulashka women — they screamed and spun away, covering their faces with their hands. "It's either really sacred ... to them, or really dangerous!"

The Grotesque, seeing the Kulashkas grind to a halt, slid over the women and made for Harkat. One of the men darted ahead of the monster and waved his arms at it, shouting at the top of his lungs. The Grotesque paused, then swatted the man aside with its huge head and fixed its gaze on us again. It was snarling now — it meant to throw itself at us and finish us off. I drew back my vial to hurl at the beast, but a woman dashed between me and the Grotesque and waved her arms like the man had. This time the monster didn't swat the Kulashka aside, but stared fiercely at her as she crooned a song and waved her arms above her head.

When she had the full attention of the Grotesque, the woman stepped away from the altar and led the beast aside. The rest of the Kulashkas filed into the gap the Grotesque had left and stared at us hatefully — but also fearfully.

"Keep your vial up!" Harkat warned me, shaking his at the Kulashkas, who flinched miserably. Following a quick conference, a few of the women chased the children out of the temple and ran after them, leaving only the men and the sturdier, more warlike women.

The chief lowered his spear and again tried to communicate, making gestures with his hands, pointing to the Grotesque, the altar and the vials. We tried making sense of his signals, but couldn't.

"We don't understand!" I shouted, frustrated. I pointed to my ears, shook my head and shrugged.

The chief cursed — I didn't need to speak his language to know that — then took a deep breath and said something to his clan. They hesitated. He barked the words again, and this time they parted, clearing a space between us and the path to the temple doorway. The chief pointed at the path, then us, then back at the path. He looked at us questioningly to see if we understood.

"You're going to … let us go?" Harkat asked, repeating the Kulashka's gestures.

The chief smiled, then raised a warning finger. He pointed to the vials in our hands, then at the cylinder behind us. "He wants us to replace the vials first," I whispered to Harkat.

"But we need the … holy liquid," Harkat objected.

"This is no time to dig your heels in!" I hissed. "They'll kill us if we don't do what they say!"

"What's to stop them killing ... us anyway?" Harkat asked. "The vials are all that's ... keeping us safe. If we abandon them, why shouldn't they ... cut us down dead?"

I licked my lips nervously, gazing at the Kulashka chief, who repeated his gestures, smiling warmly this time. I pointed to his spear when he finished. He looked at it, then tossed it away. He snapped at the rest of the Kulashkas and they too disposed of their weapons. Then they took another few steps away from us, spreading wide their empty hands.

"We have to trust them," I sighed. "Let's quit while we're ahead, put the vials back, and pray they're people of their word."

Harkat delayed for another frustrating moment, then nodded gruffly. "OK. But if they kill us on ... our way out, I'll never speak ... to you again."

I laughed at that, then stepped up to the crystal cylinder to return the vial of poison to its rightful place. As I did, a bearded man stumbled out of the shadows of the temple, waving a jug over his head and whooping loudly. "Fear not, lads! The fleet's here t' save ye!"

"Spits!" I bellowed. "No! We're sorting this out! Don't—"

I never finished. Spits raced past the chief and smashed him over the head with a long curved knife. The chief fell, screaming, blood pumping from his scalp. The other Kulashkas yelled with confusion and anger, then dived for their weapons.

"You moron!" I roared at Spits as he bounded on to the altar. "What the hell are you doing?"

"Saving ye!" the ex-pirate yelled with delight. He was weaving heavily from side to side, drunker than I'd ever seen him, his eyes barely focused. "Gimme that bottle o' pus," he grunted, snatching Harkat's vial from him. "If this is what the freaks is scared of, this is what we'll let 'em have!"

Spits raised the vial to lob at the Kulashkas. A loud shriek stopped him — the Grotesque was returning! Either the woman controlling it had been distracted by Spits's wild entrance, or she'd decided to set the beast on us. Either way, it was scampering towards us on its fingers at a frightening speed. In a couple of seconds it would be on us and the fight would be over.

Yelping with a drunken mixture of excitement and terror, Spits tossed the vial at the Grotesque. The glass missed its head, but connected with its long, fleshy body and smashed open. The instant it did, there was a huge explosion and the Grotesque and the floorboards beneath it disappeared in a spray of blood, flesh, bone and splintered wood.

The explosion blasted us from the platform and sent the Kulashkas crashing to the floor like bowling pins. I had just enough presence of mind to cradle my vial close to my chest as I fell, then tucked it inside my shirt to keep it safe as I rolled over on to my back in the aftermath of the blast. I now knew why the Kulashkas were so afraid of the vials — the Grotesque's venom was liquid explosive!

As I sat up, stunned, ears ringing, eyes stinging, I saw that the Grotesque wasn't the only casualty. Several of the Kulashkas — those who'd been closest to the monster — were lying dead on the floor. But I hadn't time to feel sorry for the Grotesque worshippers. The blast had also shattered a couple of the huge pillars supporting the roof, and as I watched, one pillar tipped over and crashed into another, which toppled into another and then another, like giant dominoes. Gazing up at the ceiling, I saw a series of cracks run across it, then huge chunks of the roof broke loose and cascaded down around the collapsing pillars. Within a matter of seconds the temple was going to fold in on itself, crushing all who lay within!

# CHAPTER NINETEEN

THOSE KULASHKAS still alive and alert to the danger fled for the doorway. Some made it to safety, but most were trapped beneath the pillars and roof, which caved in around them as they ran. Stumbling to my feet, I set off after the Kulashkas, but Harkat grabbed me. "We'll never make it!" he gasped.

"There's no other way out!" I screamed in reply.

"Have to ... shelter!" he yelled, dragging me away from the main path. He hobbled across the floorboards, his green eyes darting from left to right as he watched for falling debris.

"We're in fer it now!" Spits hollered, popping up beside us, eyes alight with crazy drunken glee. "Face the heavenly stairs and cough up yer prayers!"

Harkat ignored the ex-pirate, dodged a chunk of heavy masonry, paused, then started jumping up and down on the spot. I thought he'd lost his mind, until I saw the hole in the floor where his foot had gone through earlier. Twigging to his plan, I bounced up and down beside him on the fragile floorboards. I didn't know how deep the pit was beneath, or if we'd be safe in it, but we couldn't fare any worse below than up here.

"What in the devil's name are ye—" Spits began. He got no further, because at that point the floor gave way and the three of us plummeted into darkness, yelling wildly as we fell.

We landed in a heap several metres beneath the temple, on a hard stone floor, Spits on top of Harkat and me. Groaning, I shoved Spits off — he'd been knocked out during the landing — and looked up. I saw part of the roof give way far overhead and come crashing down. Yelping, I stumbled to my feet and dragged Spits off to one side, cursing at Harkat to follow. There was a fierce, thunderous roar at our heels as we only just cleared the section of falling roof, which exploded upon contact with the floor and showered us with splinters and chips of stone.

Coughing — the force of the impact had raised a thick cloud of dust — we pushed ahead blindly, dragging Spits between us, into darkness and what we hoped was safety from the crumbling Temple of the Grotesque. After several frantic metres we came to a hole in the ground. Exploring with my hands, I said, "I think it's a tunnel — but it drops sharply!"

"If it gets covered over ... we'll be trapped," Harkat said.

There was a heavy bang overhead and the floorboards above us creaked ominously. "We don't have a choice!" I yelled, and crawled into the tunnel, bracing myself against the walls with my hands and feet. Harkat shoved Spits after me, then came himself — the tunnel was only just wide enough to accommodate his bulky body.

We clung near the top of the tunnel a few seconds, listening to the sounds of the destruction. I peered down the tunnel, but there was no light, and no way of telling how long it was. Spits's body weighed a ton and my feet began to slip. I tried digging in with my nails but the stone was too smooth and tough. "We have to slide!" I bellowed.

"What if we can't get ... back up?" Harkat asked.

"One crisis at a time!" I shouted, and let go. I lay flat on my back, allowing my body to shoot down the tunnel. It was a short, fast ride. The tunnel dropped sharply for many metres, then gradually levelled out. I came to a stop several seconds later at the end of the tunnel, where I stretched out a foot, searching for the floor. I hadn't found it when the unconscious Spits barrelled into the back of me and sent me sprawling out into open space.

I opened my mouth to yell, but hit the ground before I could — the mouth of the tunnel was only a metre or two off the floor. Relieved, I got to my knees — and was promptly knocked flat when Spits toppled out on top of me. Swearing blindly, I pushed him off and was rising again when Harkat shot out of the tunnel and bowled me over.

"Sorry," the Little Person muttered, easing himself off. "Are you OK?"

"I feel like I've been run over by a steamroller," I groaned, then sat up and took deep breaths of the musty air, letting my head clear.

"We've escaped being crushed by ... the temple," Harkat noted after a while, as the noises echoing through the tunnel decreased and then ceased.

"For whatever good it'll be," I grunted. I couldn't see my friend in the gloom of the underground cavern. "If there's no way out, we'll face a slow, miserable death. We might wind up wishing we'd been squashed by a falling pillar."

Beside me, Spits groaned feebly, then muttered something unintelligible. There was the sound of him sitting up, then, "What's happening? Where have the lights gone?"

"The lights, Spits?" I asked innocently.

"I can't see!" he gasped. "It's pitch black!"

"Really?" I said, eager to punish him for fouling things up with the Kulashkas. "*I* can see fine. How about you, Harkat?"

"Perfectly," Harkat murmured. "I wish I had ... sunglasses, it's so bright."

"My eyes!" Spits howled. "I'm blind!"

We let Spits suffer a while, before telling him the truth. He berated us with some choice insults for scaring him, but soon calmed down and asked what our next move would be.

"I guess we walk," I answered, "and see where we end up. We can't go back, and there are walls to the left and right—" I could tell by the echoes of our voices "—so it's straight ahead until a choice presents itself."

"I blame ye fer this," Spits muttered. "If ye hadn't gone prancing about in that bloody temple, we'd be waltzing through the fields now, with all the fresh air in the world t' breathe."

"*We* weren't the ones who … tossed bombs when there wasn't a need!" Harkat snapped. "We'd agreed a deal with … the Kulashkas. They were letting us go."

"That lot?" Spits snorted. "They'd've strung ye up and had ye fer breakfast!"

"I'll string *you* up if you don't … shut your mouth," Harkat growled.

"What's eating him?" Spits asked me, stung by Harkat's tone.

"Many Kulashkas died because of you," I sighed. "If you'd stayed outside like you were supposed to, they needn't have."

"Who cares about that lot?" Spits laughed. "They ain't of our world. What's the difference if some of 'em got squished?"

"They were people!" Harkat roared. "It doesn't matter what … world they were from. We had no right … to come in here and kill them! We—"

"Easy," I hushed him. "We can't put it right now. Spits was only trying to help, in his clumsy, drunken way. Let's concentrate on finding a way out, and leave the finger-pointing for another time."

"Just keep him away … from me," Harkat grumbled, pushing to the front and taking the lead.

"That's not very polite," Spits complained. "I thought, as an imp, he'd be delighted to cause havoc."

"Be quiet," I snapped, "or I'll change my mind and set him on you!"

"Crazy pair o' landlubbers," Spits snorted, but kept further comments to himself and fell in behind me as I stumbled after Harkat.

We limped along in silence for a number of minutes, disturbed only by the sound of Spits slurping from his jug of poteen (no fear *that* got broken in the explosion!). It was completely dark in the tunnel. I couldn't see Harkat, even though he was only a metre or so ahead of me, so I concentrated on my sense of hearing, following him by sound alone. His large grey feet made a very distinctive noise, and because I was focusing on that, I didn't hear the other sounds until they were almost upon us.

"Stop!" I hissed suddenly.

Harkat came to an instant standstill. Behind me, Spits stumbled into my back. "What're ye–" he began.

I clamped a hand over his mouth, finding it with little difficulty from the stink of his breath. "Not a word," I whispered, and through the throb of his lips I felt his heartbeat pick up speed.

"What's wrong?" Harkat asked quietly.

"We're not alone," I said, straining my ears. There were very slight rustling sounds all around us, ahead, at the sides, behind. The sounds stopped for a few seconds when we stopped, but then picked up again, slightly slower and quieter than before.

"Something just crawled over my right foot," Harkat said.

I felt Spits stiffen. "I've had enough o' this," he muttered fearfully, and made to pull away and run.

"I wouldn't do that," I said softly. "I think I know what this is. If I'm right, running would be a *very* bad idea."

Spits trembled but held his nerve and stood his ground. Releasing him, I bent to the ground slowly, as gracefully as I could, and gently laid a hand on the floor of the tunnel. A few seconds later, something crawled over my fingers, something with hairy legs ... two ... four ... six ... eight.

"Spiders," I whispered. "We're surrounded by spiders."

"Is that all?" Spits laughed. "I'm not scared o' a few wee spiders! Stand aside, boys, and I'll stamp 'em out fer ye."

I sensed Spits raising a foot into the air. "What if they're poisonous?" I said. He froze.

"I've a better one," Harkat said. "Maybe these are babies. This is a world of ... giants — the Grotesque and that monstrous toad. What if there are giant ... spiders too?"

At that, I froze like Spits had, and the three of us stood there, sweating in the darkness, listening ... waiting ... helpless.

# CHAPTER TWENTY

"THEY'RE CRAWLING up my leg," Spits said after a while. He hadn't lowered his foot and was trembling wildly.

"And mine," Harkat said.

"Let them," I said. "Spits — lower your foot, as slowly as you can, and make sure you don't squash any of the spiders."

"Can you talk to them and ... control them?" Harkat asked.

"I'll try in a minute," I said. "First I want to find out if these are all we have to deal with." I'd been fascinated by spiders when I was a kid. That's how I got mixed up with Mr Crepsley, through his performing tarantula, Madam Octa. I had a gift for communicating with arachnids and had learnt to control them with my thoughts. But that had been on Earth. Would my powers extend to the spiders here?

I penetrated the darkness with my ears. There were hundreds, maybe thousands of spiders in the tunnel, covering the floor, walls and ceiling. As I listened, one dropped on to my head and began exploring my scalp. I didn't brush it off. Judging from the noise and the feel of the spider on my head, these were medium-sized tarantulas. If there were any giant spiders, they weren't moving — maybe because they were waiting for us to walk into their lair?

I carefully raised my right hand and touched my fingers to the side of my head. The spider found them a few seconds later. It tested the new surface, then crawled on to my hand. I brought my hand and the spider down and around, so that I was facing it (even though I couldn't see it). Taking a deep breath, I focused my attention on the spider and began talking to it inside my head. When I'd done this in the past, I'd used a flute to help focus my thoughts. This time I just had to wing it and hope for the best.

"Hello, little one. Is this your home? We're not intruders — we're just passing through. I can tell you're a beauty. Intelligent too. You can hear me, can't you? You understand. We're not going to harm you. We just want safe passage." As I continued talking to the spider, reassuring it of our peaceful intentions, flattering it and trying to get inside its head, I extended my range of thought and directed my words at the spiders around us. It's not necessary to control every spider in a huge pack, just those nearest to you. If you have the talent and experience, you can then use those spiders to control the rest. I could do that with spiders in my own world — were this lot the same, or were we doomed flies caught in an underground web?

After a couple of minutes, I put my abilities to the test. Bending, I let the spider crawl off my fingers on to the floor, then addressed the group around us. "We need to move on now, but we don't want to hurt any of you. You'll have to spread out of our way. We can't see you. If you stay bunched together, we won't be able to avoid you. Move, my beauties. Slip to the sides. Let us pass freely."

Nothing happened. I feared the worst but kept on trying, talking to them, urging them to part. I'd have been more authoritative with normal spiders, and ordered them out of our way. But I didn't know how these would react to direct commands, and didn't want to risk angering them.

For two or three minutes I spoke to the spiders, asking them to move. Then, when I was almost on the point of quitting and making a break for freedom, Harkat said, "They're climbing off me."

"Me too," Spits croaked a moment later. He sounded on the verge of tears.

All around us the spiders were retreating, slowly edging out of our way. I stood, relieved, but didn't break mental contact with them. I kept on talking inside my head, thanking them, congratulating them, keeping them on the move.

"Is it safe to advance?" Harkat asked.

"Yes," I grunted, anxious not to lose my concentration. "But slowly. Feel in front with your toes every time you take a step."

I went back to communicating my thoughts to the spiders. Harkat edged ahead, one sliding step after another. I followed, keeping close, maintaining my link with the spiders. Spits stumbled along behind, holding on to my sleeve with one hand, clutching his bottle of poteen to his chest with his other.

We walked for a long time in this way, many of the spiders keeping pace with us, new recruits joining them further along the tunnel. No signs of any giants. It was hard work talking to them for such an extended amount of time, but I didn't let my concentration slip.

Finally, after twenty or thirty minutes, Harkat stopped and said, "I've come to a door."

Stepping up beside him, I laid a hand on hard, smooth wood. It was covered in cobwebs, but they were old and dry, and brushed away easily at my touch. "How do you know it's a door?" I asked, momentarily breaking contact with the spiders. "Maybe the tunnel's just blocked off." Harkat found my right hand and guided it to a metal handle. "Does it turn?" I whispered.

"Only one way to ... find out," he said, and together we twisted it down. There was almost no resistance, and the door swung inwards the instant the latch was retracted. A soft buzzing noise greeted us from inside. The spiders around us scuttled backwards half a metre.

"I don't like this," I hissed. "I'll go in alone and check it out." Moving ahead of Harkat, I entered the room and found myself standing on cold, hard tiles. I flexed my bare toes a few times, to be certain.

"What's wrong?" Harkat asked when he didn't hear me moving.

"Nothing," I said. Remembering the spiders, I re-established contact and told them to stay where they were. Then I took a step forward. Something long and thin brushed against my face — it felt like a giant spider leg! I ducked sharply — the spiders had guided us into a trap! We were going to be devoured by monster arachnids! We had to run, get out, flee for our lives! We...

But nothing happened. I wasn't seized by long, hairy spider legs. There was no sound of a giant spider creeping towards me, intent on finishing me off. In fact there were no sounds at all, except for the strange buzzing and the fast, hard beating of my heart.

Rising slowly, I stretched out my arms and explored. My left hand found a long, narrow piece of cord hanging from above. Wrapping my fingers around it, I tugged softly. It resisted, so I tugged again, slightly harder. There was a click, then a harsh white light flooded the room.

I winced and covered my eyes — the light was blinding after the blackness of the tunnel. Behind me, I heard Harkat and Spits spin aside to avoid the glare. The spiders took no notice of it — living in utter darkness, they must have discarded their sense of sight some time in the past.

"Are you OK?" Harkat roared. "Is it a trap?"

"No," I muttered, spreading my fingers slightly in front of my eyes, allowing my pupils to adjust. "It's just a..." I stopped as my fingers parted. Lowering my hands, I gazed around, bewildered.

"Darren?" Harkat said. When I didn't answer, he poked his head through the door. "What's...?" He stopped when he saw what I was looking at, and stepped into the room, speechless. Spits did the same moments later.

We were in a large kitchen, like any modern kitchen back on Earth. There was a fridge – the source of the buzzing – a sink, cupboards, a bread bin, a kettle, even a clock over the table, though the hands had stopped. Closing the door to the room to keep the spiders out, we quickly searched the cupboards. We found plates, mugs, glasses, cans of food and drink (no labels or dates on the cans). There was nothing in the fridge when we opened it, but it was in full working order.

"What's going on?" Spits asked. "Where'd all this stuff come from? And what's that?" Hailing from the 1930s, he'd never seen a fridge like this before.

"I don't—" I started to answer, then stopped, my eyes falling on a saltcellar on the table — there was a piece of paper underneath, with a note scribbled across it. Removing the saltcellar, I scanned the note in silence, then read it out loud.

> "'Top of the morning to you, gentlemen! If you've made it this far, you're doing splendidly. After your narrow escape in the temple, you've earned a rest, so put your feet up and tuck into the refreshments — courtesy of this kitchen's previous owner, who never got round to enjoying them. There's a secret exit tunnel behind the refrigerator. It's a few hundred metres to the surface. After that, you face a short walk to the valley wherein lies the Lake of Souls. Head due south and you can't miss it. Congratulations on overcoming the obstacles to date. Here's hoping all goes well in the final stretch. Best regards, your dear friend and sincere benefactor — Desmond Tiny.'"

Before discussing the note, we nudged the fridge aside and checked behind it. Mr Tiny had told the truth about the tunnel, though we wouldn't know for sure where it led until we explored it.

"What do you think?" I asked Harkat, sitting and pouring myself one of the fizzy drinks from the cupboard. Spits was busy examining the fridge, oohing and aahing with wonder at the advanced technology.

"We have to do as ... Mr Tiny says," Harkat replied. "We were heading in a general ... southerly direction anyway."

I glanced at the note again. "I don't like the bit about 'here's hoping all goes well in the final stretch'. It sounds as though he thinks it *won't*."

Harkat shrugged. "He might have said that ... just to worry us. At least we know we're ... close to the—"

We were startled by a shrill cry. Leaping to our feet, we saw Spits turning away from one of the cupboards, which he'd moved on to after the fridge. He was shaking and there were tears in his eyes.

"What is it?" I yelled, thinking it must be something dreadful.

"It's ... it's..." Spits held up a bottle full of a dark golden liquid, and broke into a wet-eyed grin. "It's *whisky!*" he croaked, and his face was as awe-filled as the Kulashkas' had been when they knelt before their Grotesque god.

Several hours later, Spits had drunk himself into a stupor and lay snoring on a rug on the floor. Harkat and I had eaten a filling meal and were resting against a wall, discussing our adventures, Mr Tiny and the kitchen. "I wonder where all this ... came from?" Harkat said. "The fridge, food and drinks ... are all from our world."

"The kitchen too," I noted. "It looks to me like a nuclear fallout shelter. I saw a programme about places like this. People built underground shelters and stocked them with imperishable goods."

"You think Mr Tiny transported an entire ... shelter here?" Harkat asked.

"Looks that way. I've no idea why he'd bother, but the Kulashkas certainly didn't build this place."

"No," Harkat agreed. He was silent a moment, then said, "Did the Kulashkas remind you ... of anyone?"

"What do you mean?"

"There was something about their appearance ... and the way they talked. It took me a while to work it out ... but now I have it. They were like the Guardians of the Blood."

The Guardians of the Blood were strange humans who lived in Vampire Mountain and disposed of dead vampires in exchange for their internal organs. They had white eyes like the Kulashkas, but no pink hair, and spoke in a strange language which, now that I thought about it, did seem quite like the Kulashkas'.

"There *were* similarities," I said hesitantly, "but differences too. The hair was pink, and the eyes were a duller white colour. Anyway, how could they be related?"

"Mr Tiny might have transported ... them here," Harkat said. "Or maybe this is where the Guardians of the ... Blood originally came from."

I mused that one over for a while, then rose and walked to the door.

"What are you doing?" Harkat asked as I opened the door on to the tunnel.

"Checking out a hunch," I said, crouching low and casting about with my eyes. Most of the spiders had left but a few were still close by, hunting for food or resting. I made mental contact with one and summoned it. It crawled on to my left hand and lay snugly in my palm as I lifted it to the light and examined it. It was a large grey spider with unusual green spots. I studied it from all sides, to be absolutely certain, then set it on the floor of the tunnel and closed the door again.

"Ba'Shan's spiders," I said to Harkat. "They're the spiders Madam Octa created when she bred with Ba'Halen's spiders in Vampire Mountain."

"You're certain?" Harkat asked.

"They were named in my honour by Seba. I'm positive." I sat down again beside Harkat, my forehead creased as I picked away at the puzzle. "Mr Tiny must have brought them here, like the kitchen, so I guess he could have brought some of the Guardians of the Blood too. But Ba'Shan's spiders aren't blind and the Guardians don't have pink hair. If Mr Tiny did bring them here, it must have been decades ago in this world's time, if not longer — they'd need that long to transform."

"It seems like a lot of effort to ... go to," Harkat said. "Maybe he wanted the Guardians to build ... the Temple of the Grotesque. And the kitchen might just have ... been for a joke. But why bring the spiders?"

"I don't know," I said. "When you put them all together, they don't add up. There's something more to this, a bigger picture which we're missing."

"Maybe the answer's in the kitchen," Harkat said, rising and slowly surveying the tiles, table and cupboards. "The details are so fine. Maybe the answer is hidden ... among them." He wandered around the room, gradually winding his way over to the fridge, where several postcards were attached by magnets to the door. They were from various tourist attractions on Earth — Big Ben, the Eiffel Tower, the Statue of Liberty, and so on. I'd seen them earlier but paid no attention.

"Maybe there are clues or further ... instructions on the back of these," Harkat said, taking down one of the cards. Turning it over, he studied it in silence, then quickly grabbed another, and another.

"Anything?" I asked. Harkat didn't answer. He was gazing down at the postcards, his lips moving silently. "Harkat? Are you OK? Is something wrong?"

Harkat's gaze flicked over me, then returned to the postcards. "No," he said, tucking the cards away inside his tattered blue robes. He reached for the others.

"Can I see the cards?" I asked.

Harkat paused, then said softly, "No. I'll show them to you ... later. No point distracting ourselves now." That raised my interest, but before I could press to see the postcards, Harkat sighed. "It's a shame we don't ... have any of the holy liquid. I suppose we'll just have to..." He stopped when he saw me grin and reach inside my shirt. "No way!" he whooped.

I held up the vial I'd tucked away after being blown from the altar. "Am I brilliant or what?" I smirked.

"If you were a girl ... I'd kiss you!" Harkat cheered, rushing over.

I passed the vial to him and forgot about the postcards. "How do you think it works?" I asked as he turned the vial around, careful not to slosh the explosive liquid. "With all that force in its venom, surely the Grotesque should have blown its head off the first time it sunk its fangs into something."

"It must not be explosive ... to begin with," Harkat guessed. "Maybe an element in the air ... reacts with the poison after its release ... and changes it."

"A pretty big change," I laughed, then took the vial back. "How do you think we're supposed to use it?"

"There must be something ... we have to blow up," Harkat said. "Perhaps the Lake is covered ... and we have to blast a way through. What puzzles me more are the ... globes." He picked out one of the gelatinous globes from within his robes and tossed it up and down. "They must serve a ... purpose, but I can't for the life of ... me think what it is."

"I'm sure it'll become clear," I smiled, tucking the vial away. Pointing at the sleeping Spits, I said, "We should apologize to him when he wakes up."

"What for?" Harkat snorted. "Killing the Kulashkas and almost ... getting us killed too?"

"But don't you see? He was *meant* to. Mr Tiny wanted us to come here, but we wouldn't have if Spits hadn't barged in. Without him, we'd have no holy liquid. And even if we'd managed to sneak a vial out of the temple, we wouldn't have known about its explosive properties — we'd have blown ourselves to bits!"

"You're right," Harkat chuckled. "But I think an apology ... would be wasted. All Spits cares about now ... is his whisky. We could call him every foul ... name in the world, or praise him ... to the heavens, and he wouldn't notice."

"True!" I laughed.

We lay down after that and rested. I spent the quiet moments before sleep thinking about our adventures and the puzzle this world presented, and wondering what awful, life-threatening obstacles lay in wait for us at the end, in the valley of the Lake of Souls.

# CHAPTER TWENTY-ONE

AFTER A long sleep and a hot meal, courtesy of a small gas stove, we packed some tins and drinks (Spits made the three remaining bottles of whisky his first priority), along with a few of the longer knives, and exited the underground kitchen. I switched off the light before we left — a force of habit from the time when my mum would roar whenever I left lights on around the house.

The tunnel was a couple of hundred metres long and ended in the side of a riverbank. The exit was blocked with loose stones and sandbags, but they were easy to remove. We had to jump into the river and wade across to dry land, but the water was shallow. On the far bank we got undercover quickly and hurried away through the tall stalks of grass. We were anxious not to run into any Kulashka survivors.

It was midday when we left the kitchen. Although we'd previously travelled at night, we marched steadily all day, hidden by the tall grass. We stopped late in the night to sleep, and set off early the next morning. That evening we cleared the grasslands. We were delighted to leave the tall grass behind — we were covered in burs and insects and nicked all over from the sharp edges of the blades. The first thing we did was find a pool of water and wash ourselves clean. After that we ate, rested a few hours, then headed south, reverting to our previous pattern of walking by night and sleeping by day.

We expected to come upon the valley at every bend — Mr Tiny had said it was a short walk — but another night passed without any sight of it. We were worried that we'd taken the wrong path, and discussed backtracking, but early the next night the ground rose to a peak and we instinctively knew that our goal lay on the other side. Harkat and I hurried up the rise, leaving Spits to catch up in his own time (he'd been drinking heavily and was making slow progress). It took us half an hour to reach the top. Once there, we saw that we were at the head of the valley — and we also saw the enormity of the task ahead.

The valley was long and green, with a small lake — a glorified pond, as Mr Tiny had accurately called it — set in the centre. Apart from that, the valley was featureless — except for five dragons resting around the edge of the water!

We stood staring down into the valley at the dragons. One looked like the creature which had attacked us on the raft. Two were smaller and slimmer, probably females — one had a grey head, the other white. The remaining two were much smaller — infants.

As we studied the dragons, Spits approached, panting heavily. "Well, lads," he wheezed, "is this the valley or ain't it? If it is, let's sing a wee sea shanty t' celebrate our—"

We jumped on him before he burst into song, and smothered his startled cries. "What's going on?" he yelped through my fingers. "Are ye mad? 'Tis me — Spits!"

"Quiet!" I hushed him. "Dragons!"

He snapped out of his drunkenness. "Let me see!" We rolled off and let him wriggle forward to the edge of the overhang. His breath caught in his throat when he saw the dragons. He lay there for a minute, studying them silently, then returned to our side. "I recognize two of 'em. The biggest is the one that attacked ye in the lake by my shack. I've seen the one with the grey head too, but not the others."

"Do you think they're just ... resting?" Harkat asked.

Spits tugged on his straggly beard and grimaced. "The grass round the Lake has been trampled flat in a big wide circle. 'Twouldn't have got that way if they'd only been here a while. I think this is their den."

"Will they move on?" I asked.

"No idea," Spits said. "Mebbe they will — though I doubt it. They're safe from attack here — they'd see anything coming long before it reached 'em — and the land around is teeming with animals and birds for 'em to feed on. Plus, my lake's not far off — as the dragon flies — with all the fish they could wish fer."

"They've children too," Harkat noted. "Animals normally stay where ... they are when they're rearing their young."

"So how are we going to get to the Lake of Souls?" I asked.

"Are ye sure that *is* the Lake?" Spits asked. "It looks awful small t' be home to a load o' dead souls."

"Mr Tiny said it would be small," I told him.

"There could be another lake nearby," Spits said hopefully.

"No," Harkat grunted. "This is it. We'll just have to keep watch and ... wait for them to leave — they have to hunt ... for food. We'll move in when they go and ... hope they don't return too quickly. Now, who wants to creep forward and ... take first watch?"

"I'll go," I said, then snatched Spits's bottle from him as he made to slug back a shot. I also grabbed his sack, where his other bottles were stowed.

"Hey!" he protested.

"No more whisky until this is over," I told him. "You're taking the next watch — and you're taking it sober."

"You can't boss me about!" he griped.

"Yes I can," I growled. "This is serious business. I'm not having you fly off the handle like you did in the temple. You can have some whisky before you go on watch, and when you come off, but between those times — not a drop."

"And if I refuse?" he snarled, reaching towards his long curved knife.

"We'll break the whisky bottles," I said simply, and his face went white.

"I'd kill ye if ye did!" he croaked.

"Aaarrr," I grinned, "but that wouldn't bring yer whisky back!" Handing the bottle and sack to Harkat, I winked at Spits. "Don't worry — when we're through, you can drink all the whisky you want." Then I hurried forward to find a bush to hide behind and observe the dragons.

We kept watch for almost a week before accepting that we'd have to revise our plan. At least three dragons remained in the valley at any given time, usually the two young ones and a female, though sometimes the male took one of the youngsters hunting with him. There was no way of telling when the absent dragons would return — sometimes the male was gone overnight, while other times he'd sweep back to his family within minutes, a bleating sheep or goat clutched between his claws.

"We'll just have to ... sneak in one night and hope ... they don't spot us," Harkat said as we debated our options. We were in a rough cave we'd dug in the soil of the hill, to hide us from the dragons when they took flight.

"Them dragons have awful good eyesight," Spits said. "I seen 'em spot prey from hundreds o' feet up on nights as black as a shark's soul."

"We could try burrowing to the Lake," I suggested. "The soil isn't hard-packed — I'm sure I could dig a way through."

"And when you broke through ... to the Lake?" Harkat asked. "The water would flood the tunnel ... and we'd all drown."

"We ain't chancing that!" Spits said quickly. "I'd rather be ate by one o' them demons than drowned!"

"There must a way to get past them," I groaned. "Maybe we could use the explosive Grotesque poison — wait until they're grouped together, sneak up close and lob it among them."

"I doubt we'd be able to ... get close enough," Harkat said. "And if even one of them survived..."

"If we had more'n one vial, we'd have nowt to worry about," Spits sighed. "We could walk in and toss a vial at 'em any time they came near. Mebbe we should go back t' the temple and search fer more vials."

"No," I frowned. "That's not the answer — even if they didn't blow up during the blast, they'd be buried under rubble. But you're on to something..." I took out my vial of "holy liquid" and examined it. "Mr Tiny knew that we'd crash through the floorboards and make our way to the kitchen, so maybe he also knew we'd only grab a single vial."

"Then one must be enough," Harkat muttered, taking the vial from me. "There must be a way we can ... use it to get to the Lake."

"'Tis a pity Boom Boom Billy ain't with us," Spits chuckled. When we looked at him blankly, he explained. "Boom Boom Billy was a wonder with bombs. He knew all about dynamite and gunpowder, and how t' blow things up. The cap'n often said Billy was worth his weight in gold." Spits chortled. "Which made it all the funnier when he blew himself up trying t' crack open a chest full of ingots!"

"You've got a warped sense of humour, Spits," I sniffed. "I hope that one day you—" I stopped, eyes narrowing. "*Bombs!*" I exclaimed.

"You have an idea?" Harkat asked excitedly.

I shushed him with a wave of a hand, thinking furiously. "If we could make bombs out of the 'holy liquid'..."

"How?" Harkat asked. "We know nothing about ... bombs, and even if we did, we don't ... have anything to make them with."

"Don't be so sure about that," I said slowly. Reaching inside my shirt, I took out the piece of cloth I'd wrapped my share of the gelatinous globes in, and carefully unrolled them on to the floor. Picking up a jelly-like ball, I squeezed it softly between my fingers, watching the thin liquid within ooze from side to side. "By themselves, these globes are worthless," I said. "The 'holy liquid' is worthless too — by itself. But if we put them together..."

"Are you thinking of covering ... the globes with the liquid?" Harkat asked.

"No," I said. "It would drop off on to the ground and explode. But if we could inject it *into* the globes..." I trailed off into silence, sensing I was close to the answer, but unable to make the final leap in logic.

With a sudden grunt, Harkat beat me to the punch. "The tooth!" He dug through his robes for the bag of teeth he'd taken from the black panther.

"What're they?" Spits asked, never having seen the teeth before.

Harkat didn't answer, but sorted through them until he found the hollow tooth with the K carved on it. Holding it up, he blew through the tooth to make sure it was clear, then passed it to me, his green eyes shining brightly. "You have smaller fingers," he said.

Picking up a globe, I brought the tip of the tooth close to it, then stopped. "We'd better not try this here," I said. "If something goes wrong…"

"Agreed," Harkat said, shuffling towards the mouth of the cave. "Besides, we'll have to test them … to make sure they work. We'd best do that … out of earshot of the dragons."

"What 're ye on about?" Spits whined. "Ye ain't making sense!"

"Just follow close behind," I winked. "You'll see!"

We made our way to a copse of thick, stunted trees a few kilometres away. Once there, Harkat and Spits huddled behind a fallen trunk, while I squatted in a clearing and laid several gelatinous globes and the panther's tooth on the earth around me. With extreme care, I uncorked the vial of explosive poison. It smelt like cod-liver oil. I set the vial down, lay out flat on my stomach and placed one of the globes directly in front of me. With my left hand, I gently jabbed the sharp, narrow end of the panther's tooth into the globe. When it was sticking in half a centimetre, I picked up the vial with my right hand, brought its lip to the rim of the tooth, and poured.

I was sweating furiously as the first drops trickled into the tooth — if they exploded this close to my face, I was dead meat. But, like treacle, the liquid rolled slowly down the hole inside the tooth, then into the soft gelatinous globe.

I filled the tooth to the top – it didn't hold very much – then removed the vial and waited for all the liquid to seep into the globe. It took a minute, but eventually the globe had absorbed all of the deadly poison from the tooth.

Keeping my hands steady, I removed the tip of the tooth from the top of the globe and held my breath, watching the jelly-like material close over the tiny hole, until it was no more than a pinprick in the skin of the globe. Once it had closed as far as it was going to, I corked the vial, set the tooth aside, and stood. "It's done," I called to Harkat and Spits.

Harkat crept over. Spits stayed where he was, eyes wide, hands over his head. "Take the vial and tooth," I told Harkat. "Lay them where Spits is, so they're out of harm's way."

"Do you want me to ... come back to help?" Harkat asked.

I shook my head. "I can throw it further than you. I'll test it myself."

"But you're a half-vampire," he said. "You took a vow never to use ... missile-firing weapons or bombs."

"We're on another world — as far as we know — and facing a bunch of dragons — I think this qualifies as an exceptional circumstance," I said dryly.

Harkat grinned, then swiftly retreated with the vial, my share of the globes and the panther's tooth. When I was alone, I crouched, took hold of the poison-filled globe, and cautiously picked it up. I winced as my fingers tightened around the globe, expecting it to blow up in my face — but it didn't. I turned the globe over, to see if any of the liquid spilt out. Detecting no leaks, I stood, swung my arm back, then lobbed the globe at a gnarly tree in the distance.

The instant the globe was out of my hand, I ducked and covered my head with my hands, following the globe's flight through the cracks between my fingers. It soared cleanly ahead, before connecting with the tree. When it hit the trunk, the shell of the globe smashed, the liquid splashed with great force over the wood, and the air was rent with the sound of a sharp explosion. My fingers snapped closed and I buried my face in the ground. When, a few seconds later, I raised my head and opened my eyes, I saw the top half of the tree topple over, torn to shreds in the middle.

Getting up slowly, I studied the shattered tree, then turned and smiled at Harkat and Spits, who were also on their feet. Taking a cheeky bow, I hooted, "Move over Boom Boom Billy — there's a new kid in town!"

Then Harkat and Spits were racing towards me, whooping with excitement, eager to make some bombs of their own.

# CHAPTER TWENTY-TWO

EARLY AFTERNOON the next day. We'd been waiting for the male dragon to go hunting. Ideally, we'd like to have waited until he took one of the females or young dragons with him, but he usually only made short trips when accompanied. Our best bet was to make our move when he was off hunting by himself, in the hope that he wouldn't return while we were in the valley.

Finally, near the end of my watch, the dragon unfurled his long wings and took to the sky. I hurried off to alert Harkat and Spits.

We'd filled the remaining thirty-two globes with liquid from the vial. The vial was still about a third full, and I carried it in my shirt, keeping it in reserve. Harkat and I had divided the globes between us, giving none to Spits, even though he'd argued bitterly for a share. There were two reasons why we kept the globes from him. Firstly, it was our aim to scare off the dragons, not kill them. Neither of us wished to destroy such mystical, marvellous creatures, and we couldn't trust Spits not to go bomb-happy. The second reason was that we needed him to concentrate on fishing. The pirate had held on to his net, despite all we'd been through – he had it wrapped around his chest – and he was the best qualified to fish for Harkat's soul. (We weren't sure what form the souls in the Lake would take, or how we'd recognize Harkat's, but we'd worry about that when – if! – we got there.)

"Ready?" I asked, crawling out of our makeshift cave, four small globes cradled in my hands.

"Ready," Harkat said. He was carrying six of the globes — his hands were bigger than mine.

"Aaarrr," Spits growled, still sour about not being given any bombs. He'd been in a foul mood most of the week, due to the tiny amount of whisky we'd limited him to.

"When this is over," I tried to cheer him up, "you can drink all the whisky you like and get steaming drunk, OK?"

"I like the sound o' that!" he chuckled.

"Are you looking forward to … getting home?" Harkat asked.

"Home?" Spits frowned, then grinned sickly. "Aaarrr. 'Twill be great. I wish we was there already." His eyes shifted nervously and he looked away quickly, as though he'd been caught stealing.

"We'll go in three abreast," I told Spits, shuffling to the top of the hill. "You take the middle. Head straight for the Lake. We'll protect you."

"What if the dragons don't flee from the bombs?" Spits asked. "Will ye let 'em have it in the gob?" Spits thought we were crazy for not wanting to blow up the dragons.

"We'll kill them if we have to," I sighed. "But only if there's no other way."

"And only after they've ... eaten you," Harkat added, then laughed when Spits cursed loudly at him.

Forming a line, we checked ourselves one last time. Harkat and I were carrying everything we owned in our pockets, and Spits had his sack slung over his shoulder. Taking deep breaths, we shared crooked grins, then started down into the valley, where the four dragons were waiting.

A young dragon spotted us first. It was playing with its sibling — the pair often chased each other around the valley, like two overgrown kittens. When it saw us, it drew up short, flapped its wings and screeched warningly. The heads of the female dragons shot up, their hot yellow eyes fierce above their long purple faces.

The female with the grey head got to her feet, spread her wings, flapped them firmly and soared into the air. She circled around, screeching, then directed her snout at us and zoomed in. I could see her nostrils expanding as she prepared to blow fire.

"I'll deal with this one," I called to Harkat, stepping forward and holding up one of the larger globes. I judged my moment finely, waited until the dragon was almost directly overhead, then threw the globe hard into the earth and ducked. It exploded, sending soil and pebbles flying up into the dragon's face. She screamed with panic and veered sharply away to the left.

The second female took to the air at the sound of the explosion, and the young dragons followed, adopting a position several metres above their mothers, who hovered side by side.

While the dragons hung in the air, we hurried towards the Lake of Souls, Harkat and I watching our every footstep, all too aware of the consequences if we stumbled and smashed the deadly globes. Spits was muttering over and over, "Better be worth it! Better be worth it! Better be..."

The female dragons split up and attacked us on two fronts at the same time, swooping out of the sky like a couple of comets. Harkat and I waited, then threw our globes at the same time, confusing the dragons with loud explosions and blinding geysers of earth and stones.

The dragons dogged our steps all the way to the Lake, attacking in turn or together every minute or so, only pulling clear when we launched our globes. One of the young dragons tried to join in, but its mother shot a warning streak of fire at it, frightening it back to its previous safe height.

As we progressed, I realized the dragons were intelligent creatures. After the first few explosions, they no longer flew into the blasts but pulled up short as soon as they saw us lobbing the globes. On a couple of occasions I tried to outfox them by just pretending to toss a globe, but they obviously saw through my ploy and only withdrew when I actually launched one.

"They'll keep coming until we run out of globes!" I roared at Harkat.

"Looks that way!" Harkat yelled back. "Have you been keeping track ... of how many you've used?"

"I think seven or eight."

"Me too," Harkat said. "That only leaves us with about ... half our original supply. Enough to get us to the ... Lake — but not to get back!"

"If we're going to retreat, we'll have to do it now," I noted.

To my surprise, Spits answered before Harkat could. "No!" he yelled, his face alight. "We're too close t' pull back!"

"Spits seems to be getting into the spirit of the adventure," I laughed.

"The time he picks to ... develop a backbone!" Harkat snorted in reply.

We hurried on to the Lake and arrived a couple of minutes later, having used another two globes. The female dragons pulled away when they saw us draw up to the edge of the Lake. They hovered in the air with their children, high above our heads, observing suspiciously.

Spits was the first to gaze into the water of the Lake of Souls, while Harkat and I kept a watch on the dragons. After a few seconds he fell to his knees and moaned softly. "It's beautiful! All I ever dreamt, and more!"

Staring over my shoulder to see what he was babbling about, I found myself gazing into murky blue water, in which swam hundreds upon hundreds of shimmering human figures. Their bodies and faces were pale and ill defined, some swelling out and sucking in, almost like a fish puffing itself up and returning to its normal size. Others were squashed into tiny balls or stretched out to impossible lengths. All swam in slow, mournful circles, listless, oblivious to distractions, their blinking eyes or flexing fingers the only signs that they weren't totally lifeless. A few of the shapes drifted towards the upper levels of the Lake every now and then, but none broke the surface of the water. I got the impression that they couldn't.

"The souls of the dead," Harkat whispered. Both of us had turned our backs on the dragons, momentarily captivated by the spectacle of the Lake.

Most of the figures twisted slowly as they swam, so that their faces revolved in and out of sight. Every face was a picture of loneliness and sorrow. This was a lake of misery. Not agony – nobody seemed to be in pain – just sadness. I was studying the faces, filled with a sense of pity, when I spotted one I knew. "By the black blood of Harnon Oan!" I shouted, taking an involuntary step back.

"What is it?" Harkat asked sharply — he thought I'd found the person he used to be.

"*Murlough!*" It was less than a breath on my lips. The first vampaneze I ever encountered. Consumed by madness, he'd lost control and had been killing people in Mr Crepsley's home city. We'd tracked him down and Mr Crepsley killed him. The vampaneze looked exactly the way he had when he died, only his purple sheen was muted by the water of the Lake and the depth he was swimming at.

As I watched, Murlough sunk downwards, slowly dropping from sight into the lower reaches of the Lake. A shiver ran down my spine. I'd never thought to look upon

Murlough's face again. It had dredged up many bad memories. I was lost in thought, transported to the past, reliving those long ago nights, wondering what other souls I might find here. Not Mr Crepsley — Evanna had told me his soul was in Paradise. But what about the first vampaneze I'd killed? Gavner Purl? Arra Sails? Kur–

"Beautiful," Spits murmured, breaking my train of thought. He looked up at me and his eyes were wet with happy tears. "The little man in the green galoshes told me 'twould be like this but I never believed it till now. "All my dreams would come true", he said. Now I know he wasn't lying."

"Never mind your dreams!" I snapped, recalling the danger we were in. I put Murlough from my thoughts and spun to keep both eyes on the dragons. "Get fishing, quick, so we can get out of here!"

"I'll get fishing, sure enough," Spits giggled, "but if ye thinks I'm leaving this pool o' sunken treasures, ye're crazier than them Kulashkas!"

"What do you mean?" Harkat asked, but Spits didn't answer immediately, only unravelled his net with measured care and fed it into the still water of the Lake of Souls.

"I was considered a prize on the *Prince o' Pariahs*," the pirate said softly. "Nobody cooked as fine a meal as Spits Abrams. The cap'n used to say I was second in importance only t' Boom Boom Billy, and when Billy blew himself up, I became the most valuable man aboard. Every pirate would've sold his mother fer a bowl o' Spits's famous stew, or a slice of his delicious roast meat."

"He's cracking up!" I yelled.

"I don't think so," Harkat said nervously, studying Spits as he focused on his net, lips drawn back over his teeth, eyes burning with a frightening inner light.

"They never asked where the meat came from," Spits continued, swishing his net through the water. The souls in the Lake parted and swam around the net automatically, but their glum expressions didn't change. "Even when we'd been at sea fer months on end, and all the other supplies had run out, I was able t' slap up as much meat as they could eat."

The pirate paused and his mouth grew tight with anger. "When they found out, they said I wasn't human and didn't deserve t' live. But they knew. Deep down, they must've guessed, and they went on chewing regardless. 'Twas only when a new man caught me and made a fuss that they had to admit it. Hypocrites!" he roared. "They was a stinking bunch o' lying, double-faced hypocrites, fit only t' roast in the fires o' hell!"

Spits's face grew crafty and he laughed maniacally, drawing his net out, checking its condition, then lowering it back into the water. "But since the devil couldn't be bothered with 'em, I'll treat 'em to a fire of me own. Aaarrr! They thought they'd seen the last o' Spits Abrams when they tossed me overboard. But we'll see who has the last laugh when they're draped on a spit, sizzling slowly over my flames!"

"What's he talking about?" I croaked.

"I think I understand," Harkat whispered, then spoke to Spits. "How many of the people ... that you fished from the sea ... did you *kill*?"

"Most of 'em," Spits giggled. "In the heat o' battle, nobody took any notice of them what jumped overboard. I kept the occasional one alive, t' show off t' the cap'n and crew. But I slit the throats o' most and hid the bodies in the galley."

"And then you carved them ... up, cooked them and served them ... to the pirates," Harkat said hollowly, and I felt my stomach churn.

"*What?*" I gasped.

"That's Spits's big secret," Harkat said sickly. "He was a cannibal and he turned his ... crewmates into cannibals too!"

"They loved it!" Spits howled. "They'd've gone on eating Spits's grub fer ever and said nowt if that new lad hadn't walked in on me while I was carving up a nice fat vicar and his wife! After that, they acted disgusted and treated me like a monster."

"I've eaten human flesh," Harkat said quietly. "Little People will eat anything. When I first came back from the dead, my thoughts ... weren't my own, and I ate with the rest. But we only ate the flesh ... of those who'd died naturally. We didn't kill. And we didn't take pleasure ... from it. You *are* a monster, even to someone ... like me."

Spits sneered. "Come off it, imp! I know why ye're really here — t' feast yer chops on Spits's stew! Shan boy too!" His eyes fixed on me and he winked crookedly. "Ye thought I didn't know what ye was, but Spits ain't as dumb as he lets on. Ye're a bloodsucker! Ye fed from me when ye thought I was asleep. So don't play the innocents, lads — 'twon't work!"

"You're wrong, Spits," I said. "I drink blood to survive, and Harkat's done things in the past that he's ashamed of.

But we aren't killers or cannibals. We don't want any part of your unholy feast."

"We'll see if ye think that way when ye smell the cooking," Spits cackled. "When yer lips are drooling and yer bellies growling, ye'll come running, plates out, begging fer a thick, juicy slice o' thigh."

"He's completely out of his mind," I whispered to Harkat, then called aloud to Spits. "Have you forgotten the dragons? *We'll* get roasted and eaten if we stand around gabbing!"

"They won't bother us," Spits said confidently. "The Tiny man told me. He said as long as I stayed within eight feet o' the Lake, the dragons couldn't harm me — they can't come this close. There's a spell on the Lake. Unless a living person jumps or falls in, the dragons can't come near."

Spits stopped dragging on his net and gazed at us calmly. "Don't ye see, lads? We don't ever need t' leave. We can stay here the rest of our lives, fishing fer dinner each day, all the water we can drink. Tiny said he'd drop by if we made it, and promised t' provide me with pots and material t' build fires. We'll have t' eat our catch raw till then, but I've ate humans raw before — not as tasty as when cooked, but ye won't have cause fer complaint."

"*That's* your dream!" Harkat hissed. "Not to return to our world, but to stay ... here for ever, fishing for the souls ... of the dead!"

"Aaarrr!" Spits laughed. "Tiny told me all about it. The souls don't have bodies in the water — them's just ghosts that we see. But once they're dragged on to dry land, they become real, the way they was before they died. I'll be able t' kill 'em again and carve 'em up any way I like. An unending supply — including the souls o' the cap'n and most o' the others on the *Prince o' Pariahs*! I can have revenge on top of a full stomach!"

There was a heavy thud behind us — the male dragon had returned and set down close to where we were standing. I raised a globe to throw at him, but then I saw that he wasn't coming any closer. Spits was right about the dragons not being able to approach the Lake.

"We can't let you do it," I said. Focusing on Spits, I started walking towards him.

"Ye can't stop me," he sniffed. "If ye don't want t' stay, ye can leave. I'll fish up the imp's soul and ye can take yer chances with the dragons. But there's nowt ye can do t' make me go with ye. I'm staying."

"No," I said. "We won't let you."

"Stay back!" Spits warned, lowering his net and drawing a knife. "I like ye both – ye're decent sorts fer a vampire and an imp! – but I'll slice the skin clean off yer bones if I have t'!"

"Don't try, Spits," Harkat said, stepping up behind me. "You've seen us in action. You know we're stronger and faster … than you. Don't make us hurt you."

"I ain't scared o' ye!" Spits shouted, backing away, waving his knife at us. "Ye need me more than I need ye! Unless ye back off, I won't fish yer soul out, and this'll all have been fer nowt!"

"I don't care," Harkat said softly. "I'd rather blow my chance … and die, than leave you here to torment the souls … of the dead and feed upon them."

"But they're bad 'uns!" Spits howled. "These ain't the souls o' good people — they're the souls o' the lost and damned, who couldn't get int' heaven."

"It doesn't matter," Harkat said. "We won't let you ... eat them."

"Crazy pair o' landlubbers," Spits snarled, coming to a halt. "Ye think ye can rob me o' the one thing that's kept me going all these years alone in this hellhole? 'Twasn't enough fer ye t' rob me o' me whisky — now ye wants t' take me meat away too! Well damn ye, demons o' the dark — damn ye both t' hell!"

With that shrill cry, Spits attacked, slicing wildly with his knife. We had to leap back quickly to avoid being gutted by the raging ex-pirate. Spits raced after us, whooping gleefully, chopping with his knife. "Gonna slice ye up and cook ye!" he howled. "The dead can wait — I'll feast on *yer* flesh tonight! I'm gonna see what ye're made of inside. I never ate a vampire or imp before — 'twill make fer an interesting comparison!"

"Spits!" I roared, ducking out of the way of his knife. "Stop now and we'll let you live! Otherwise we'll have to kill you!"

"Only one man'll be doing any killing today!" Spits retorted. "Spits Abrams, scourge o' the seas, lord o' the Lake, sultan o' chefs, king o'—"

Before Spits got any further, Harkat slid inside his stabbing range and grabbed his knife arm. Spits screamed at the Little Person and punched him with his free fist. When that didn't have any effect, he pulled a whisky bottle out of his sack and prepared to break it over Harkat's head.

"No you don't!" I grunted, seizing Spits's forearm. I squeezed tightly, until I heard bones cracking. Spits screeched painfully, dropped the bottle and spun away from me. I released him and he retreated sharply, breaking free of Harkat's grip, collapsing on the ground a couple of metres away.

"Quit it!" I yelled as Spits staggered to his feet and drew another bottle, cradling his injured arm across his chest.

"Never!" he cried. "I've still got one good hand. That'll be enough t'–" He stopped when he saw us freeze, our eyes widening. "What're ye up t' now?" he asked suspiciously. We couldn't answer, only gaze wordlessly at the space behind him. Spits sensed that we weren't trying to trick him, and whipped around to see what we were staring at. He found himself gazing up into the fierce cold eyes of the male dragon.

"Is that all that's bothering ye?" Spits hooted. "Didn't I tell ye they couldn't come next nor near us as long as we stayed..."

He trailed off into silence. He looked down at his feet, then at us, then at the Lake — which was about four or five metres away from where he was standing!

Spits could have made a run for it, but didn't. With a bitter smile, he shook his head, spat into the grass, and muttered, "*Aaarrr!*" The dragon opened its mouth wide when Spits said that – as though he'd been awaiting an order – and blew a huge ball of fire over the stranded ex-pirate. Spits disappeared in flames and Harkat and I had to cover our eyes and turn aside from the heat.

When we looked again, a fiery Spits was stumbling towards us, arms thrashing, face invisible beneath a mask of red flames. If he was screaming, we couldn't hear him over the crackle of his burning hair and clothes. We lunged out of his way as Spits staggered closer. He continued past us, oblivious to our presence, and didn't stop until he reached the edge of the Lake of Souls and toppled in.

Snapping out of our daze, we raced to the Lake in case there was anything we could do to help Spits. But we were too late. He was already deep under water, arms still moving, but weakly. As we watched, the shimmering shades of the dead surrounded the pirate's body, as though guiding it on its way. Spits's arms gradually stopped waving, then his body sunk deeper into the water, until it vanished from sight in the murky gloom of the soul-filled depths.

"Poor Spits," Harkat croaked. "That was awful."

"He probably deserved it," I sighed, "but I wish it could have happened some other way. If only he'd—"

A roar stopped the words dead in my throat. My head shot around and I spotted the male dragon, hovering in the air close above us, eyes gleaming. "Don't worry," Harkat said. "We're close to the Lake. It can't..." The words died on his lips and he stared at me, his green eyes filling with fear.

"The spell!" I moaned. "Spits said it would only last until a living person fell into the Lake! And he was still alive when..."

As we stood trembling, the dragon — no longer bound by the spell — opened his jaws wide and coughed a ball of fire straight at us — meaning to finish us off the same way he'd killed Spits!

# CHAPTER TWENTY-THREE

I REACTED quicker to the flames than Harkat — I'd been badly burnt many years earlier, and had no wish to suffer the same fate again. I hurled myself into the Little Person, knocked him clear of the blast and rolled after him. As the flames zipped past us, out over the water of the Lake – momentarily illuminating the faces of the dead trapped within – I reached for a globe and hurled it at the ground beneath the dragon. There was a large explosion and the dragon peeled away, roaring — this was his first exposure to our explosives.

"Hurry!" I shouted at Harkat. "Give me your globes, grab the net and fish your soul out!"

"I don't know how ... to fish!" Harkat howled.

"There's no better time to learn!" I bellowed, then threw another globe as one of the females swooped upon us.

Harkat swiftly unloaded his globes and laid them on the ground by my feet. Then, grabbing Spits's abandoned net, he pulled it out of the Lake, paused a moment to clear his thoughts, and slowly fed the net in. As he did, he muttered softly, "I seek my soul, spirits ... of the dead. I seek my soul, spirits ... of the dead. I seek my—"

"Don't talk!" I yelled. "Fish!"

"Quiet!" Harkat hissed. "This is the way. I sense it. I must call upon my soul to ... lure it into the net."

I wanted to ask how he'd figured that out, but there was no time — the male and both females were attacking, the females from the left and right, the male floating out over the Lake, in front of us. Scaring off the females with two hastily thrown globes, I studied the dragon angling down towards the surface of the Lake. If I threw a globe at the Lake, it wouldn't burst. That meant I'd have to aim for the dragon itself, and possibly kill him. It seemed a shame, but there were no other options.

I was getting a fix on the dragon when an idea struck me. Hurling the globe out on to the water in front of the approaching beast, I grabbed a nearby pebble, took careful aim, and sent it flying at the globe. It struck just as the dragon was nearing the globe, showering the creature's face with a seething funnel of water.

The dragon pulled out of its attack and arced away into the air, screeching its frustration. The females almost sneaked in while I was dealing with the male, but I spotted them just in time and scattered them with another blast. While the dragons regrouped overhead, I did a quick globe count — eight remained, plus the vial.

I wanted to tell Harkat to hurry, but his face was knitted together fiercely as he bent over the net, whispering softly to the souls in the Lake, searching for the soul of the person he used to be. To disturb him would be to delay him.

The dragons attacked again, in the same formation as before, and once again I successfully repelled them, leaving myself with five lonely-looking globes. As I picked up three more, I considered aiming to kill — after these three, I'd be down to my final pair — but as I studied the dragons circling in the air, I was again struck by their awesome majesty. This was their world, not ours. We had no right to kill them. What if these were the only living dragons, and we wiped out an entire species just to save our own necks?

As the dragons attacked once more, I still wasn't sure what I intended to do with the explosive globes. Clearing my mind, I allowed my self-defence mechanism to kick in and make the choice for me. When I found my hands pitching the globes short of the dragons, scaring them off but not killing them, I nodded grimly. "So be it," I sighed, then called to Harkat, "I can't kill them. After the next attack, we're done for. Do you want to take the globes and—"

"I have it!" Harkat shouted, hauling ferociously on the net, the strings of which tightened and creaked alarmingly. "A few more seconds! Buy me just a ... few more seconds!"

"I'll do what I can," I grimaced, then faced the dragons, which were homing in on us as before, patiently repeating their previous manoeuvre. For the final time I sent the females packing, then pulled out the vial, tossed it on to the surface of the Lake, and smashed it with a pebble. Some glass must have struck the male dragon when the vial exploded, because he roared with pain as he peeled away.

Now that there was nothing else to do, I hurried to Harkat and grabbed hold of the net. "It's heavy!" I grunted, feeling the resistance as we tugged.

"A whopper!" Harkat agreed, grinning crazily.

"Are you OK?" I roared.

"I don't know!" he shouted. "I'm excited but terrified! I've waited so long … for this moment, and I still … don't know what to expect!"

We couldn't see the face of the figure caught in the strands of the net – it was turned away from us – but it was a man, light of build, with what looked to be dirty blond hair. As we pulled the spirit out of the Lake, its form glittered, then became solid, a bit at a time, first a hand, then an arm, followed by its other hand, its head, chest…

We had the rescued soul almost all the way out when I caught sight of the male dragon zooming towards us, his snout bleeding, pain and fury in his large yellow eyes. "Harkat!" I screamed. "We're out of time!"

Glancing up, Harkat spotted the dragon and grunted harshly. He gave the net one last desperate tug. The body in the net shot forward, its left foot solidifying and clearing the water with a pop similar to a gun's retort. As the dragon swooped down on us, its mouth closed, nostrils flaring, working on a fireball, Harkat spun the body over on to its back, revealing a pale, confused, horrified face.

"What the–?" I gasped.

"It can't be!" Harkat croaked, as the man in the net — impossibly familiar — stared at us with terror-filled eyes.

"Harkat!" I roared. "That can't be who you were!" My gaze flicked to the Little Person. "Can it?"

"I don't know," Harkat said, bewildered. He stared at the dragon — now almost upon us — then down at the man lying shivering on the shore. "Yes!" he shouted suddenly. "That's me! I'm him! I know who I was! I..."

As the dragon opened its mouth and blew fire at us with all the force it could muster, Harkat threw his head back and bellowed at the top of his voice, "I was the vampire traitor — *Kurda Smahlt!*"

Then the dragon's fire washed over us and the world turned red.

# CHAPTER TWENTY-FOUR

I FELL to the ground, clamping my lips and eyes shut. Clambering to my knees, I tried to crawl out of the ball of fire before I was consumed to the bone—

—then paused when I realized that although I was surrounded by the dragon's flames, there wasn't any heat! I opened my left eyelid a fraction, ready to shut it again quick. What I saw caused both my eyes to snap open and my jaw to drop with astonishment.

The world around me had stopped. The dragon hung frozen over the Lake, a long line of fire extending from its mouth. The fire covered not just me, but Harkat and the naked man – *Kurda Smahlt!* – on the ground. But none of us was burnt. The static flames hadn't harmed us.

"What's going on?" Harkat asked, his words echoing hollowly.

"I haven't a clue," I said, running a hand through the

frozen fire around me — it felt like warm fog.

"Over ... there!" the man on the ground croaked, pointing to his left.

Harkat and I followed the direction of the finger and saw a short, tubby man striding towards us, beaming broadly, playing with a heart-shaped watch.

"*Mr Tiny!*" we shouted together, then cut through the harmless flames – Harkat grabbed Kurda under the arms and dragged him out – and hurried to meet the mysterious little man.

"Tight timing, boys!" Mr Tiny boomed as we came within earshot. "I didn't expect it to go that close to the wire. A thrilling finale! Most satisfying."

I stopped and stared at Mr Tiny. "You didn't know how it would turn out?" I asked.

"Of course not," he smirked. "That's what made it so much fun. A few more seconds and you'd have been toast!"

Mr Tiny stepped past me and held out a cloak to Harkat and his naked companion. "Cover the poor soul," Mr Tiny punned.

Harkat took the cloak and draped it around Kurda's shoulders. Kurda said nothing, just stared at the three of us, his blue eyes wide with suspicion and fear, trembling like a newborn baby.

"What's going on?" I snapped at Mr Tiny. "Harkat can't have been Kurda — he was around long before Kurda died!"

"What do you think, Harkat?" Mr Tiny asked the Little Person.

"It's me," Harkat whispered, studying Kurda intensely. "I don't know how ... but it is."

"But it can't—" I began, only for Mr Tiny to interrupt curtly.

"We'll discuss it later," he said. "The dragons won't stay like this indefinitely. Let's not be here when they unfreeze. I can control them normally, but they're in quite an agitated state and it would be safer not to press our luck. They couldn't harm me, but it would be a shame to lose all of you to their fury at this late stage."

I was anxious for answers, but the thought of facing the dragons again enabled me to hold my tongue and follow quietly as Mr Tiny led us out of the valley, whistling chirpily, away from the lost remains of Spits Abrams and the other dead spirits held captive in the Lake of Souls.

Night. Sitting by a crackling fire, finishing off a meal which two of Mr Tiny's Little People had prepared. We were no more than a kilometre from the valley, out in the open, but Mr Tiny assured us that we wouldn't be disturbed by dragons. On the far side of the fire stood a tall, arched doorway, like the one we'd entered this world by. I longed to throw myself through it, but there were questions which needed to be answered first.

My eyes returned to Kurda Smahlt, as they had so often since we'd pulled him out of the Lake. He was extremely pale and thin, his hair untidy, his eyes dark with fear and pain. But otherwise he looked exactly as he had the last time I saw him, when I'd foiled his plans to betray the vampires to the vampaneze. He'd been executed shortly afterwards, dropped into a pit of stakes until he was dead, then cut into pieces and cremated.

Kurda felt my eyes upon him and glanced up shamefully. He no longer shook, though he still looked very uncertain. Laying aside his plate, he wiped around his mouth with a scrap of cloth, then asked softly, "How much time has passed since I was put to death?"

"Eight years or so," I answered.

"Is that all?" He frowned. "It seems much longer."

"Do you remember everything that happened?" I asked.

He nodded bleakly. "My memory's as sharp as ever, though I wish it wasn't — that drop into the pit of stakes is something I'd rather never think about again." He sighed. "I'm sorry for what I did, killing Gavner and betraying the clan. But I believed it was for the good of our people — I was trying to prevent a war with the vampaneze."

"I know," I said softly. "We've been at war since you died, and the Vampaneze Lord has revealed himself. He..." I gulped deeply. "He killed Mr Crepsley. Many others have died as well."

"I'm sorry," Kurda said again. "Perhaps if I'd succeeded, they'd still be alive." He grimaced as soon as he said that, and shook his head. "No. It's too easy to say 'what if' and paint a picture of a perfect world. There would have been death and misery even if you hadn't exposed me. That was unavoidable."

Harkat hadn't said much since we'd sat down — he'd been studying Kurda like a baby watching its mother. Now his eyes roamed to Mr Tiny and he said quietly, "I know I was Kurda. But *how*? I was created years before ... Kurda died."

"Time is relative," Mr Tiny chuckled, roasting something that looked suspiciously like a human eyeball on a stick over the fire. "From the present, I can move backwards into the past, or forward into any of the possible futures."

"You can travel through time?" I asked sceptically.

Mr Tiny nodded. "That's my one great thrill in life. By playing with time, I can subtly influence the course of future events, keeping the world on a chaotic keel — it's more interesting that way. I can help or hinder humans, vampires and vampaneze, as I see fit. There are limits to what I can do, but I work broadly and actively within them.

"For reasons of my own, I decided to help young Master Shan," he continued, addressing his words to Harkat. "I've laid many plans around that young man, but I saw, years ago, that he was doomed for an early grave. Without someone to step in at vital moments — for instance, when he fought with the bear on his way to Vampire Mountain, and later with the wild boars during his Trials of Initiation — he would have perished long ago.

"So I created Harkat Mulds," he said, this time speaking to me. He swallowed the eyeball he'd been cooking and belched merrily. "I could have used any of my Little People, but I needed someone who'd cared about you when he was alive, who'd do that little bit extra to protect you. So I went into a possible future, searched among the souls of the tormented dead, and found our old friend Kurda Smahlt."

Mr Tiny slapped Kurda's knee. The one-time General flinched. "Kurda was a soul in agony," Mr Tiny said cheerfully. "He was unable to forgive himself for betraying his people, and was desperate to make amends. By becoming Harkat Mulds and protecting you, he provided the vampires with the possibility of victory in the War of the Scars. Without Harkat, you would have died long ago, and there would have been no hunt for the Lord of the Vampaneze — he would simply have led his forces to victory over the vampires."

"But I didn't know ... that I used to be Kurda!" Harkat protested.

"Deep down you did," Mr Tiny disagreed. "Since I had to return your soul to the past, I had to hide the truth of your identity from you — if you'd known who you were, you might have tried to directly interfere with the course of the future. But on a subconscious level, you knew. That's why you fought so bravely beside Darren, risking your life for his on numerous occasions."

I thought about that in silence for a long while, as did Harkat and Kurda. Time travel was a difficult concept to get my head around, but if I overlooked the paradox of being able to send a soul from the future into the past to alter the present — and didn't question how it was achieved — I could see the logic. Kurda had betrayed the vampires. Ashamed, his soul remained bound to Earth. Mr Tiny offered him the chance of redemption — by returning to life as a Little Person, he could make amends for his foul deeds.

"There's something I don't understand," Kurda said, then winced. "Actually, there's *loads* I don't understand, but one thing in particular. My plan to betray the vampires would have succeeded if Darren hadn't interfered. But you say

Darren would have died without my aid as Harkat Mulds. So, in effect, I helped Darren mastermind my own downfall!"

Mr Tiny shook his head. "You would have perished regardless of the outcome. Your death was never in question — merely the manner of it."

"What puzzles *me* the most," Harkat muttered, "is how ... the two of us can be here at the same ... time. If I'm Kurda and he's ... me, how can we exist together?"

"Harkat's wiser than he looks," Mr Tiny noted with a chuckle. "The answer is that you *can't* — at least, not for very long. While Kurda remained in the Lake of Souls, Harkat was free to roam the world. Now that Kurda has emerged, one must make way for the other."

"What do you mean?" I asked sharply.

"Kurda and Harkat share the same soul," Mr Tiny explained, "but while a soul can be split, it can only lay claim to one body at any given time — although there *are* ways to protect a newly formed body for a while, if you send it into the past, which is how Harkat was previously able to function at the same time as Kurda." As the original, Kurda has a natural claim to existence. Even now, the strands of Harkat's form are unravelling. Within a day his body will dissolve, releasing his share of their soul. A split soul can never be rejoined — Harkat and Kurda are two different people. Since this is the case, Harkat's half of their soul must depart this world. It's nature's way."

"You mean Harkat's going to die?" I yelled.

"He's dead already," Mr Tiny chuckled.

"Stop splitting hairs!" I growled. "Will Harkat perish if we stay here?"

"He'll perish wherever you are," Mr Tiny replied. "Now that Kurda's soul has been given form, only he has the power to spare Harkat's body."

"If I can save Harkat, I will," Kurda said immediately.

"Even if it costs you your own newly restored life?" Mr Tiny asked slyly.

Kurda stiffened. "What are you talking about?"

Mr Tiny stood and stretched. "There's much I can't tell you," he said. "But I'll explain as best I can. There are two ways in which I can create a Little Person — from a soul's resurrected body — the one which forms when a person is fished from the Lake of Souls — or from their corpse. With Harkat, I used Kurda's original remains."

"But Kurda's body was burnt to ashes," I interrupted.

"No," Mr Tiny said. "When I decided to use Kurda's soul, I returned to the time of his death and convinced the Guardians of the Blood to switch his body with another's. I used Kurda's bones to make Harkat. The deal I then made with him was that in return for his new body, he'd travel with Darren and protect him, and later, if he did as instructed, I'd free his soul — he wouldn't have to return to the Lake.

"Well, Harkat has performed admirably and is most deserving of his reward. If Kurda chooses, he can walk away a free man now. He can live out the rest of his renewed life, however long or short that proves to be. Harkat's body will fall apart, his soul will be freed, and I'll have upheld my end of the bargain."

"To live again!" Kurda whispered, eyes bright.

"*Or*," Mr Tiny added with cruel relish, "we can strike a new deal and Kurda can sacrifice himself."

Kurda's eyes narrowed. "Why would I do that?" he snapped.

"You and Harkat share a soul, but it's a soul which I have helped divide into two parts. If you let me destroy your new body, your part of your shared spirit will depart this realm instead of Harkat's. Harkat will become your soul's sole physical vessel. I can't guarantee him immunity from the Lake of Souls in that case, but he may return home with Darren and live out his life. His future will be his own — if he lives a good life and dies well, the Lake will have no claim on him."

"That's a despicable choice to present me with," Kurda growled.

"I don't make the laws," Mr Tiny shrugged. "I just obey them. One of you can live — the other must bid farewell to life. I could make the call and just kill one of you, but wouldn't you rather decide for yourselves?"

"I suppose," Kurda sighed, then looked at Harkat and grinned. "No offence, but if we were to decide on the basis of good looks, I'd win hands down."

"And if we judged it ... on loyalty," Harkat responded, "*I* would win, since I have ... never betrayed my friends."

Kurda grimaced. "Would you want to live?" he asked Harkat. "The Lake is a hellish place. Mr Tiny's offering you a guaranteed escape. Maybe you want to take it?"

"No," Harkat said. "I don't want to let go ... of life. I'd rather go back with Darren and take my chances."

Kurda looked at me. "What do you reckon, Darren?" he asked softly. "Should I grant Harkat life or set his soul free?"

I started to answer but Harkat cut in. "Darren has nothing to do ... with this. Much of my memory – *your* ... memory – is returning. A lot is clear now. I know you the same way I ... know myself. You always went your own way ... even to the point of betraying your people ... when you thought it was for their best. Be the man in death that ... you were in life. Decide for yourself."

"He put that quite well," Mr Tiny murmured.

"Couldn't have said it better myself," Kurda agreed, grinning sickly. Standing, he turned in a complete, slow circle, studying the dark world beyond the light of the fire, thinking deeply. Then he sighed and faced Mr Tiny. "I've had my fill of life. I made my choices and accepted the consequences. This is Harkat's time. I belong to death — let it have me."

Mr Tiny smiled strangely, almost warmly. "Your decision makes no sense to me but I admire you for it. I promise your death will be swift and painless, and your departure for whatever glories or terrors which lie beyond will be instant."

Mr Tiny stepped over to the arched doorway. He held up his heart-shaped watch and it glowed a deep red colour. Within seconds the doorway and the small man's face were glowing too. "Through you go, boys — the home fires are burning and your friends are waiting."

"Not yet!" I shouted. "I want to know where we are and how Evanna got here and why you stocked that kitchen underground and where the dragons came from and why—"

"Your questions must wait," Mr Tiny stopped me. His face was glowing red and he looked more frightening than anything we'd faced during the course of our journey. "Go now, or I'll leave you here to the dragons."

"You wouldn't!" I snorted, but I was in no position to call his bluff. Walking to the doorway, followed by Harkat, I stopped and gazed back at Kurda Smahlt, about to face death for the second time. There was so much I wanted to say to him, so much I wanted to ask him. But there was no time. "Thank you," I whispered simply.

"Yes — thank you," Harkat added.

"What's a life between friends?" Kurda laughed, then grew serious. "Make it count. Lead a good life, so you'll have no regrets when you die. That way your soul will fly free, and you won't be at the beck and call of meddlers like Desmond Tiny."

"If not for we meddlers, who would hold the fabric of the universe together?" Mr Tiny countered. Then, before we could pursue the conversation any further, he barked, "You must go now — or stay for ever!"

"Goodbye, Kurda," Harkat said numbly.

"Farewell, *Sire*," I saluted him.

Kurda didn't answer, just waved shortly and turned his head aside. I think he was crying. And then, leaving many questions unanswered, but having successfully achieved what we set out to, Harkat and I turned away from the living corpse, the Lake of Souls, the dragons, the Grotesque and other creatures of this twisted place, and walked through the glowing doorway, back to the world of our own.

# CHAPTER TWENTY-FIVE

MR TALL was waiting for us when we stepped through the doorway, standing beside a fire much like the one we'd left behind, close to the vans and tents of the Cirque Du Freak, but separated from the campsite by a row of trees. His small mouth was stretched into a smile as he stepped forward to shake our hands. "Hello, Darren. Hello, Harkat. I'm delighted about your safe return."

"Hello, Hibernius," Harkat greeted the Cirque owner — it was the first time he'd ever called him that.

"Ah!" Mr Tall beamed. "Your mission was a success — as Kurda, you always called me Hibernius."

"Good to see you again ... old friend," Harkat said. His voice hadn't changed, but he somehow sounded different.

As we sat around the fire, I asked where our other friends were. Mr Tall told us most were sleeping — it was late and everyone was tired after that night's performance.

"I've known for the last week that you were due to return – if you managed to make it back alive – but I wasn't sure of the exact date. I've been making a fire and waiting beside it for several nights. I could wake the others, but it would be better to wait and announce your return in the morning."

We agreed to let our friends slumber. Harkat and I began telling Mr Tall about our adventures in the mysterious world through the glowing doorway (which crumbled to ash shortly after we stepped through). Mr Tall was fascinated and listened in rapt silence, asking virtually no questions. We only meant to tell him the highlights – and save the majority of the tale for when we had more listeners – but once we started, we couldn't stop, and over the next few hours we told him all that had happened. The only time he interrupted was when we mentioned Evanna — he stopped us there and asked a lot of questions about her.

There was a long silence at the end, as the three of us stared into the dying embers of the fire and thought about our battles and narrow escapes, the fate of the deranged Spits Abrams, the wondrous dragons, the great revelation and Kurda's unenviable choice.

"Will Mr Tiny really kill Kurda?" I asked after a while.

Mr Tall nodded sadly. "A soul can divide but it cannot share two bodies. But Kurda made the right choice — Harkat will remember most of what Kurda experienced while alive, and in that way Kurda will live on. Had Kurda chosen life, all of Harkat's memories would have been lost to the world. This way they both win."

"A cheery thought to end on," Harkat said, smiling. He yawned and stared up at the moon. "How much time has passed since … we were away?"

"Time has been the same for us as for you," Mr Tall said. "Some three months have slipped by. It is summer now."

"Any news about the War of the Scars?" I asked.

"None," Mr Tall said shortly.

"I hope Debbie and Alice reached Vampire Mountain," I muttered. During my months away, I'd only rarely stopped to wonder what was happening back home. Now I was anxious to catch up on all that I had missed.

"I wouldn't trouble myself if I were you," Mr Tall said, seeing the questions in my eyes. "This is where you and Harkat are meant to be right now. The War of the Scars will find you again when destiny decrees. For the time being, relax and enjoy this calm between the storms."

Mr Tall stood and smiled at us. "I'll leave you now. Get as much sleep as you need — I'll see that you are not disturbed." As he turned to leave, he paused and glanced back at Harkat. "It would be wise to wear your mask again, now that the air is no longer safe."

"Oh!" Harkat gasped. "I forgot!" Digging out a mask, he tied it around his mouth, breathed through it a few times to make sure there weren't any rips, then lowered it so that he could speak clearly. "Thanks."

"Don't mention it," the tall man chuckled.

"Mr Tall," I said quietly, as he turned to leave again. "Do you know where we were? Was that world a different planet, the past, an alternate reality?"

The Cirque owner said nothing and didn't look back — just shook his head and hurried on towards the camp.

"He knows," I sighed. "But he won't tell."

Harkat grunted. "Did you bring anything ... back with you?" he asked.

"Only my clothes," I said. "And I don't plan on hanging on to these rags — they can go straight in the bin!"

Harkat smiled, then rifled through his robes. "I still have the postcards I took ... from the underground kitchen, as well as ... the panther's teeth." He spilt the teeth on to the grass and turned them so all the letters were face up. He idly began arranging them to form his name, but as he got to the end of "Harkat", he stopped, quickly scanned all the teeth, and groaned.

"What's wrong?" I asked sharply.

"Remember Mr Tiny saying at the ... start that we'd find a clue to who I was ... when we killed the panther?" Harkat quickly rearranged the letters on the teeth to form another name — *KURDA SMAHLT!*

I stared at the letters, then groaned like Harkat had. "The answer was in front of us all along — your name's an anagram! If we'd spent more time on the letters after we'd killed the panther, we could have solved the puzzle and skipped the rest of the ordeal!"

"I doubt it would have been ... that simple," Harkat laughed. "But at least I now know where ... my name came from. I used to wonder ... how I'd picked it."

"On the subject of names," I said, "are you sticking with Harkat Mulds or reverting to your original name?"

"Harkat Mulds or Kurda Smahlt," Harkat muttered, and said the names a few more times. "No," he decided. "Kurda's the person I used ... to be. Harkat's the person I've become. We are the same in some ways ... but different in many others. I want to be known ... as Harkat."

"Good," I said. "It would have been very confusing otherwise."

Harkat cleared his throat and looked at me oddly. "Now that you know the truth ... about me, does it change anything? As Kurda, I betrayed you and ... all the vampires. I killed Gavner Purl. I will understand if you don't ... think as highly of me as you ... did before."

"Don't be stupid," I grinned. "I don't care who you used to be — it's who you *are* that matters. You've long made up for any mistakes in your previous life." I frowned. "But does this change how *you* feel about *me*?"

"What do you mean?" Harkat asked.

"The reason you stuck by me before was that you needed my help to find out who you were. Now that you know, maybe you'd like to head off and explore the world by yourself. The War of the Scars isn't your battle any longer. If you'd rather go your own way..." I trailed off into silence.

"You're right," Harkat said after a couple of thoughtful moments. "I'll leave first thing in ... the morning." He stared seriously at my glum features, then burst out laughing. "You idiot! Of course I won't go! This is my war as much as ... it's yours. Even if I hadn't been a ... vampire, I wouldn't leave. We've been through too much ... together to split up now.

Maybe when the war is over … I'll seek a path of my own. For the time being I still feel … bound to you. I don't think we're meant … to part company yet."

"Thanks," I said simply. It was all that needed to be said.

Harkat gathered up the panther's teeth and put them away. Then he studied the postcards, turned one over and gazed at it moodily. "I don't know if I should … mention this," he sighed. "But if I don't, it will … gnaw away at me."

"Go on," I encouraged him. "Those cards have been bothering you since you found them in the kitchen. What's the big mystery?"

"It has to do with … where we were," Harkat said slowly. "We spent a lot of time wondering where … we'd been taken — the past, another world … or a different dimension."

"So?" I prodded him when he stalled.

"I think I know the answer," he sighed. "It ties it all together, why … the spiders were there … and the Guardians of the Blood, if that's … who the Kulashkas really were. And the kitchen. I don't think Mr Tiny put the kitchen … there — I think it was in place … all along. It was a nuclear fallout shelter, built to … survive when all else fell. I think it was put to the test … and it passed. I hope I'm wrong, but I'm … afraid I'm not."

He passed a postcard to me. On the front was a picture of Big Ben. There was writing on the back, a typical tourist's account of their holiday — "Having a great time, weather good, food fab." The name at the bottom and the name and address on the right-hand side of the postcard meant nothing to me.

"What's the big deal?" I asked.

"Look at the postmark," Harkat whispered.

What I saw confused me. "That date can't be right," I muttered. "That's not for another twelve years."

"They're all like that," Harkat said, passing the rest of the postcards to me. "Twelve years ahead ... fifteen ... twenty ... more."

"I don't get it," I frowned. "What does it mean?"

"I don't think we were in the past or ... on a different world," Harkat said, taking the postcards back and tucking them away. He stared at me ominously with his large green eyes, hesitated a moment, then quickly mumbled the words which turned my insides cold. "I think that barren, monster-filled wasteland ... was the *future!*"

TO BE CONTINUED...

WHO WILL BE THE

# LORD OF THE SHADOWS

READ ON FOR A SNEAK PREVIEW...

As I was stacking several chairs away, to be removed to a truck by other hands, Mr Tall stepped forward. "A moment, please, Darren," he said, removing the tall red hat he wore whenever he went on stage. He took a map out of the hat – the map was much larger than the hat, but I didn't question how he'd fitted it inside – and unrolled it. He held one end of the map in his large left hand and nodded for me to take the other end.

"This is where we are now," Mr Tall said, pointing to a spot on the map with his right index finger. I studied it curiously, wondering why he was showing me. "And this is where we will be going next," he said, pointing to a town one hundred and sixty kilometres away.

I looked at the name of the town. My breath caught in my throat. For a moment I felt dizzy and a cloud seemed to pass in front of my eyes. Then my expression cleared. "I see," I said softly.

"You don't have to come with us," Mr Tall said. "You can take a different route and meet up with us later, if you wish."

I started to think about it, then made a snap gut decision instead. "That's OK," I said. "I'll come. I want to. It … it'll be interesting."

"Very well," Mr Tall said briskly, taking back the map and rolling it up again. "We depart in the morning."

With that, Mr Tall slipped away. I felt he didn't approve of my decision, but I couldn't say why, and I didn't devote much thought to it. Instead, I stood by the stacked-up chairs, lost in the past, thinking about all the people I'd known as a child, especially my parents and younger sister.

Harkat limped over eventually and waved a grey hand in front of my face, snapping me out of my daze. "What's wrong?" he asked, sensing my disquiet.

"Nothing," I said, with a confused shrug. "At least, I don't think so. It might even be a good thing. I..." Sighing, I stared at the ten little scars on my fingertips and muttered without looking up, "I'm going home."